C

DATE DUE

JASON'S WOMEN

JEAN
DAVIES
OKIMOTO

JASON'S
WOMEN

Joy Street Books
Little, Brown and Company

Boston • Toronto

FIRST EDITION

Library of Congress Cataloging-in-Publication Data

Okimoto, Jean Davies.
  Jason's women.

  Summary: Awkward and shy, sixteen-year-old Jason
finds self-confidence and a new purpose in his lonely
life when he answers a job ad and meets eighty-year-old
Bertha Jane Fillmore and the young Vietnamese refugee girl
who is staying with her.
  [1. Friendship—Fiction. 2. Aged—Fiction.
3. Self-confidence—Fiction. 4. Vietnamese Conflict,
1961-1975—Refugees—Fiction]
I. Title.
PZ7.0415Jas   1986   [Fic]   85-28655
ISBN 0-316-63809-9

10 9 8 7 6 5 4 3 2

Joy Street Books are published by Little, Brown and Company (Inc.)

BP

Published simultaneously in Canada

PRINTED IN THE UNITED STATES OF AMERICA

In loving memory of my friend
Lola Ham Minifie
1942–1985

Acknowledgments

I would like to thank Jeff Bird,
Than-Ha Ho, Vera Ing, and Norm Rice
for helping with Jason.

J.D.O.

JASON'S WOMEN

CHAPTER 1

AFTER last night's disaster with Karen Jacobsen all I wanted to do this morning was hole up, hang out in my room — and not be bothered by anyone. It was Saturday morning and I was sitting around in my underpants, scratching the hairs on my chest (I have five of them), and trying to recover by reading the ads all these women put in the personal column in the *Weekly*. Reading the personal column never fails to cheer me up when life has dealt me a bad hand, like it did last night.

The *Weekly* is this local Seattle paper that's mailed to our house. My mother subscribed to it and it still comes to our house addressed to her even though she moved out about eight months ago. I really get off on reading the personal column. It's fantastic imagining all these wonderful women out there advertising for men. So far I haven't found any ads from women who desire a romantic, sensitive, caring, sixteen-year-old male — but I keep reading. This morning one ad really caught my eye:

> IMMATURE, IMPULSIVE, uninhibited woman, 36, professional, trim, petite. Want to join my post-divorce, adolescent-like rebellion? Bring dirty jokes, cheap wine, chocolate. PO Box 94132, Tacoma, WA 98494.

Most of the ads specify the age of the guy they want but this one didn't. This lady wanted an adolescent-like rebellion — I wonder what she'd do if a *real* adolescent showed up? If someone like me showed up with dirty jokes, cheap wine, and chocolate? I was thinking about this when the phone rang. Damn. Somehow, I knew it would be old Bert. He's my boss at Wendy's. He hadn't put me on the schedule so I didn't have to work that morning like I do most Saturdays. I was enjoying not having to put on the blue-and-white-striped Wendy's shirt and that terrible hat they make you wear to go and cut up lettuce, which is about all I get to do there. I hate cutting up lettuce. I put down the paper to answer the phone.

"Hello?"

"Jason?"

"Yeah."

"Can you come in to work? Mike called in sick and I gotta have someone here."

"Oh."

"Jason?"

"Yeah?"

"Well? Can you?"

"I guess so."

"Well, get over here as fast as you can — the whole salad bar has to be prepped."

"Okay."

I hung up the phone and then I got a pen and circled the post-divorce, adolescent-like rebellion ad. I carefully folded the *Weekly* and I put it under my bed with the pile of all these other issues that I've saved. Don't get the wrong idea — it's not that I'm hiding them. I mean, I don't have to keep that stuff under my bed. My dad never snoops around in my room and no one else goes in there because no one else lives here. It's just him and me. My room is in the basement of our house. He never gets near it. Actually, he doesn't get near the whole house much because he's always out with some woman. It seems like it's a different one each week. I can't keep track of 'em all.

I pulled on my black slacks that I had left on the back of the chair. That's the rest of the Wendy's outfit — black slacks. As I zipped my pants, I wondered why I hadn't told old Bert that I had plans. I could have said, "No way, Bert. I was just walkin' out the door. I got plans. Sorry, man." I could have just said that and then hung up. How would Bert ever know that I was just sitting around in my underpants? I mean the guy doesn't have X-ray eyes or anything. He can't see through the phone.

As I looked around on the top of my bureau for my Wendy's name tag, I stared at my face in the mirror. I am a tall guy, skinnier than I'd like to be in spite of these weights I have. I have a terrific Joe Weider

5

Weight Set but all I can press is 85 pounds, maybe 100, if I'm lucky — not exactly what you'd call Olympic material. After I work out I always check out the bod in the mirror but it always looks like the same old set of bones. I have dark hair like my dad, and brown eyes. This girl in my homeroom, Georgette Hector, told me her best friend, Karen Jacobsen, thought I was good-looking and wanted to go out with me. But do you think I ever did anything about it? No. She was the one who finally had to make the first move, and I'll tell you why. It's for the same reason that I didn't tell old Bert that I had plans today. The cold, hard, naked truth is — I'm a wimp.

My real problem is that I can't talk to people. A lot of kids have trouble talking to parents, or to teachers — stuff like that. But I have trouble talking with almost everyone. I do fine with animals — dogs, cats, birds, you name it — just not people. It's not that I don't know any words, or that I stutter. In fact, I think of all kinds of things I'd like to say, but when people talk to me, I lose it. I'm like a jock who chokes in a big game. All that flows from my mouth are dazzling things like, "I guess so," or "I don't know," or "Maybe." I've got those clever phrases down, no problem.

My older brother, Jeff, can talk great. He's in law school at the University of Michigan. You have to talk to be a lawyer. And my dad, Jack Kovak, has this business he owns — Kovak's Kans. They're these outdoor toilets that they have at construction sites and places like that. My dad says he's the Toilet

King of the Pacific Northwest. No shit, that's what he calls himself. Toilet King. Hard to believe, isn't it? My dad says he outsells Sanikan and Johnny-on-the-Spot two to one. He can talk.

Not being able to talk much doesn't mean that I don't have any friends. I hang around with these three guys in my neighborhood, Chris Weber, Dave Horowitz, and Kenny Newman. Chris, Dave, and Kenny do most of the talking when we're together and I don't say much — except when I'm one-on-one with Kenny. He's probably the only person I can talk to a little — besides myself (which I do all the time).

Kenny and I have been friends since the first grade when we went trick-or-treating and my bag broke and he gave me half his candy. He was that kind of guy — still is, for that matter. In third grade my dad put a Kovak Kan in the back yard for us. We turned it into a hideout. We never used it for its intended purpose, we just hid things down the hole. In sixth grade we had some *Playboy* magazines Kenny ripped off from his dad. We called the hideout the Porno-Potty that year. We also read Tintin books a lot along with *Playboy*. I still read Tintin sometimes, although I wouldn't admit it to a lot of people. I guess reading them reminds me of the good old days hanging out in the Kovak Kan with Kenny Newman. I don't see as much of Kenny now. Ever since the beginning of the year he's been spending all his time with Stephanie Greene. She's this fantastic looking red-headed sophomore. They do everything together. He walks her to almost every class, they have the same lunch period — they go out for lunch somewhere and eat in his car (eating lunch is probably not the only activity going on in that car; pause for heavy breathing here, folks) — *and*, if that weren't enough, he's on the phone with her every night.

Kenny and I used to do stuff on the weekends, but now, of course, every weekend he's over at Stephanie's. It seems like the only time I see the guy anymore is if there's some reason he can't be with her. When a guy gets a girlfriend, why does he have to dump the guys he used to hang around with? I wish things were like they used to be.

I found my name tag from under a bunch of junk I had left on top of my bureau. You have to wear your name tag at Wendy's. It says JASON right on top of the face of this freckle-faced kid with red hair in pigtails. (I guess this person is supposed to be Wendy.) As I pinned it on I thought, so what if I didn't have any plans and all I was doing today was reading the personal column? I'd rather do that than cut up lettuce. But it's always the same. I just seem to go along with stuff. Passive, that's what I am, passive. A total wimp.

I like to think that if I could talk to people better, that would just fix the whole problem. In my life I spend a lot of time thinking about what I wished I had said to people. Also a *lot* of time imagining what I wished other people had said to me. I spend a lot of time doing this, a hell of a lot of time. It was like that with my parents' divorce.

It just sort of happened. Last spring my mother said to me, "Jason, I've wanted a divorce from your father for quite some time, but I wanted to wait until you and Jeff were grown up. Now that you're almost through with high school . . . well, you're not a little boy anymore, Jason, and I don't see much point in my just waiting around until you graduate." And that was it. The next weekend she was gone. She moved into a houseboat with this architect guy named Roger Albright, who my dad calls "That Fruitcake."

That was it, that was the whole thing. I was hoping that there might be a big deal, a huge custody fight might have been nice. I could just see it. We would be in this awesome courtroom, and my father and my mother would each have tons of lawyers. I mean, megalawyers, whole armies of them. The lawyers would march in carrying nice leather briefcases. My father would yell, "Over my dead body will you take my son!" I would be sitting in the middle with my own court-appointed lawyer. His arm would be around my shoulder. Or maybe it would be a lady, yes, I think a lady lawyer in a nice dress would be good. She would have this great body under her dress, and her hand would rest gently on my arm. I would be wearing a suit, a dark blue suit and a shirt my mother had bought me, and a tie, a twenty-five-dollar silk tie, that my father had bought me. I would appear calm. My mother would break down in hysterics, sobbing, saying, "My boy, my boy, you can't have my boy!" The judge would pound his gavel and yell, "Order, order! Order in the court. You must control yourself, Mrs. Kovak."

However, the truth is that at this very moment my mother is probably sitting on the deck of the houseboat having a nice brunch, eating croissants — she's very big on croissants — and sipping champagne with Roger Albright. And my dad — I know where he is. He's playing golf with some lady. As I thought about his dates, I decided to look at the personal column again. I got the *Weekly* out from under my bed and I looked at the page where I had circled the adolescent-like rebellion. Right under it, I saw another ad that looked good, too.

> TOUCH OF CLASS. Blue-eyed brunette, 5'6", enjoys quality lifestyle, seeks single male who's caring, affectionate, has sense of humor, and enjoys life. My interests include dancing, movies, restaurants, Seahawks, travel, plus more. Nonsmoker. Reply PO Box 374, Seattle 98125

I don't know where my father gets these ladies he's always with. I don't think he sends in for them because he never reads the *Weekly*. He calls it "that pansy paper your mother used to take." Actually, the *Weekly*'s about the only thing that's left of Mom around here. I wondered — if she still lived here would last night's disaster have turned out differently? Maybe Mom could have cured me.

Last night was going to be my moment. I had a date with Karen Jacobsen. No, I never did ask her out — but she asked me! Our high school has girl-ask-guy dances called Tolos. I have no idea why they're called that, but the girl drives, takes you out to dinner, and pays for the dance, the whole nine yards. The guy doesn't have to do anything — definitely my kind of event. I had been in a state of shock ever since Karen asked me two weeks ago.

I was walking out of homeroom and she walked next to me.

"What class do you have next, Jason?"

"Uh — history."

"I have P.E. I hate having it first thing in the morning. It seems like I just got dressed for school and then I just have to get undressed." She laughed and her gigantic blue eyes crinkled up.

I immediately pictured her getting undressed. My face got red. I looked down at the floor.

I thought she'd leave for the gym, but as I headed toward my locker she was still bouncing along next to me. Karen Jacobsen is very bouncy. She has short curly brown hair. Everything about her seems to bounce. She talks a lot, too. Just the kind of girl I like because I don't have to worry about saying much. When I stopped at my locker, she stopped there with me.

"Are you going to the Tolo, Jason?"

"Uh — nope —"

"I'd love it if you'd go with me." She smiled up at me.

I stared at her. My brain stalled and my mouth hung open.

"Well, would you?"

I froze.

"Jason?"

"Yes!" I croaked, finally getting my mouth in gear.

For the past two weeks after school, when I wasn't working at Wendy's, I practiced my moves, dancing around in the basement in front of MTV. I also went to Elliott Bay Book Store and bought a book called *How to Fascinate Women*. I leafed through it and it had chapters on "What Women Want Most from Men" and "75 Lines Women Want to Hear." Also, to further enhance my conversation with Karen Jacobsen, I got a book called *5000 One and Two Liners for Any and Every Occasion*. On the cover it said:

> No one can resist a good laugh, and when you unload some of the explosive material in this arsenal of amusement, you'll bowl everyone over! Whether you're giving a speech or just chatting with friends, you can liven things up and win people's admiration with some of the witty sayings and humorous definitions that Leopold Fechtner, the Curator of the Library of Humor, gives on every conceivable subject.

I also leafed through *The Joy of Sex*, which I really wanted to buy, but an acute attack of embarrassment prevented me from taking this joyous book to the check-out counter.

I studied the two books I bought like I was trying to pass my driver's test or the SATs. (More embarrassment here, folks, but this was my first real date. I'm sixteen.)

How to Fascinate Women had some pointers on kissing. It said to place your hands on the woman's shoulders, gaze deeply into her eyes, turn your head slightly to avoid nose-bumping, and then tenderly touch your lips to hers while slipping your arms around her and pulling her toward you. I got the pillow from my bed and held it against the wall, pressing the corners like shoulders, then I cocked my head to avoid nose-bumping, and tenderly touched it with my lips. It seemed to go okay. I tried it a few more times, standing with the pillow against the wall with my face buried in it.

"Karen," I whispered.

"What're you doin', Kovak?"

"Huh!" I spun around. The pillow plopped to the floor.

"Your dad was getting home when I drove up. He said you were here." Kenny came in my room. "What're you doin' with that pillow?"

"Smell this thing, would ya? There's something wrong with it." I threw it at him.

Kenny caught it and smelled it. "I don't smell anything."

"Duck shit."

"What?"

"Duck shit. It smells like duck shit. I think when they got the duck feathers to make this pillow some of 'em had duck shit on 'em."

"You're crazy. I don't smell anything." Kenny threw the pillow back.

I sniffed it again. "Hmmm. Well, maybe not." I tossed it on my bed.

"Listen, Jason, I stopped by to tell you there's a party at Jensen's after the dance. Why don't you and

Karen come with us — Stephanie and I can meet you at the dance."

"Great. We'll meet you there." I went to the corner of my room and scooped up my football and tossed it to him. "Hey, Kenny, want to go to the park and throw it around a little?"

"Some other time, man, I gotta go over to Stephanie's," he said, tossing it back. I should have figured.

After Kenny left, I decided I'd had enough kissing practice so I went back to working on conversation, practicing one liners.

The morning of the dance Karen went over to the pencil sharpener in homeroom and stopped by my desk.

"I'll pick you up at seven o'clock, okay, Jason?"

I tried to remember one of my 5000 one liners for every occasion but the only one I could think of on the subject of driving was, "The most dangerous part of the car is the nut that's holding the steering wheel." Then I remembered that in *How to Fascinate Women* it advised the man to say, "I can't wait to dance with you tonight and hold you in my arms," while tenderly brushing the woman's cheek with the back of his hand.

"Jason? I said, I'll pick you up at seven o'clock, okay?"

"Yeah."

"See you then."

"Okay."

Maybe I'd do better tonight, I thought, as Karen walked back to her seat. It's hard to tenderly brush someone's cheek with the back of your hand when they're standing at the pencil sharpener and you're trapped at your desk.

That afternoon, during my last class, I started to feel weird. I broke out in a cold sweat and my stomach was churning. When I got home from school, I threw up.

"Calm yourself, Kovak," I said.

"What if I'm really sick?"

"It's just nerves 'cause its your first time out of the gate as Studly Cooldude."

"What if it's the flu, or some horrible disease?"

"Take it easy, it's probably nothing."

"What if I throw up on Karen Jacobsen!"

"Mellow out, man."

I lay down and tried to relax but in a few minutes I had to throw up again. My whole life I've had this stupid nervous stomach. I wished Mom was around — she might know what to do. I tried to call her on the phone, but there was no answer. I thought of calling her at work, but I didn't want to bother her. When she left she said she thought I was grown up and could take care of myself. I remember that every time I wish she was around.

At 6:15 I was still throwing up. I knew I'd have to call Karen and tell her I couldn't go. Before I picked up the phone, I leafed through *5000 One and Two Liners for Any and Every Occasion* but I couldn't find any to fit the occasion of barfing before a date. Then I frantically thumbed through the other book. I figured out what I would say and practiced it, saying it

15

out loud while I dialed her number and heard the phone ringing. "Karen, some bad news. I've come down with the flu and I'm not going to be able to dance for a while. But if you'd like to get your beautiful self over here to lay a cool hand on my brow, I'm certain your Florence Nightingale number would have me cured maybe in time for the last set."

"Hello."

"Uh — Karen?"

"Yes."

"This is Jason."

"Hi, Jason."

"I threw up."

"What?"

"I threw up."

"You mean you're sick, Jason? You got sick?"

"Yeah. I got sick. I can't go to the dance."

"Oh no. I mean, well I'm really disappointed. And, well, that's too bad you're sick."

"Yeah."

"Do you have the flu or something?"

"Yeah."

"Well, I guess we'll just have to try it some other time."

"Yeah."

"I hope you feel better."

"Thanks."

She sounded real sad when she got off the phone. When I hung up I went in the bathroom and spent the evening in there. Maybe I really did have the flu. But in the morning I knew it had just been my stomach up to its usual tricks, because I felt fine. Physically, that is. Mentally (until I started reading the personal column) I felt lousy. I felt like I'd lost my best friend. Actually, I've felt that way ever since Kenny started going with Stephanie Greene. That was another reason I'd been looking forward to going out with Karen last night — meeting up with Kenny and Stephanie. I was sure I could do more stuff with Kenny if I had a girl to be with.

I looked at my watch. Bert would be pissed if I didn't get to work pretty soon. I put the paper back under the bed and left. Halfway up the basement stairs, I had to go back. I'd forgotten the hat. I went back and got it, but I didn't put it on. I never put it on until I get to work. There's no point in walking around in public like that.

While I was getting the hat the phone rang again. It was Kenny.

"Hello."

"Hey, Kovak, where were you last night?"

"I got sick."

"Really?"

"Yeah. I threw up when I got home after school and it lasted most of the night."

"What d'ya tell Jacobsen?"

"I called her and told her I was sick."

"Well, I wondered what had happened when I didn't see you there. You missed a great party afterward at Jensen's house. There was a keg. His parents were out of town."

"Wish I'd been there."

"Want to go to the Huskies game today? Stephanie's with her parents, her uncle's visiting."

"I gotta work."

"Jason, do you think getting sick was like when you used to throw up before our soccer games when we were on the Mt. Baker Bombers?"

"Maybe. But Mom used to put this cold towel on my head and by game time I was ready to play. I tried everything last night and nothing worked."

"Too bad."

"Yeah, well sorry I gotta work today."

"No problem, Jason. Catch you later."

I hung up the phone and left for work again, hoping Saturday would go better than Friday. I was sick of things going wrong.

CHAPTER 2

WHEN I got to Wendy's, Bert was flying around, all bent out of shape. Old Bert's like that. He's this real jittery guy. Actually, Bert's probably only thirty but he seems old, you know how some people decay earlier than others. He has this stringy blond hair, and watery blue eyes that bug out when he's extra jittery. His face also gets red splotches on it around his nose. Bert was all uptight even though there was no one in the place. No customers, I mean. Jill and Henry were in the back. Jill Washington is a junior at my school, Ingraham High. She's black, and really pretty. She looks wonderful in the Wendy's outfit and you know a person has a great body if they look good in that. Even the hat looks good on her. I've never talked to her much. Can you believe that? We've worked together at this same Wendy's for a year and I've hardly said more than two words to her. It's pitiful. Henry is Henry Ramos. He goes to some Catholic school. Henry is shorter than me but very muscular. I don't think he has a Joe Weider Weight Set, either. Henry just grew that way with natural muscles. Henry and Jill talk a lot and I just hang around and listen (of course).

Jill was cutting up tomatoes for the salad bar and Henry was getting the meat out of the refrigerator and putting it next to the grill. You know, I've worked here almost a year, as I mentioned, and I still think it's not right to have square hamburgers. But do you think I'd ever say something about it? No.

I signed in on the time sheet and headed to the back where we prep the stuff for the salad bar.

I knew that's what Bert would want me to do. He always has me on lettuce. I guess I must just have that look or something. He sees a guy like me and he just thinks "lettuce."

"Jason!" Bert yelled as I walked behind the counter and headed toward the back.

"Yeah?"

"Cut up the lettuce."

"Okay." See what I mean? I went back to the big walk-in refrigerator and got an armload of lettuce heads and carried them to the sinks in the back. They were cold and a little bit slimy. I put them on the counter near the tomatoes Jill was cutting.

"Hi, Jason."

"Hi." I looked at Jill for a minute and then started washing the lettuce.

"You're working for Mike?"

"Yeah."

"He calls in sick all the time, but it's just 'cause he's been out partying the night before. He's too hung over to come to work."

"Yeah, maybe," I said as I started to chop the lettuce.

"Bert ought to fire that boy," Henry said. He was opening the bun boxes.

"He sure should," Jill said to Henry, while I chopped.

"Too bad you had to come in, Jason."

"Yeah." I liked it that Henry sounded sympathetic. I loaded the chopped-up lettuce into a bowl and listened to the two of them talk.

"No one comes in this place this early Saturday morning anyway," Jill said to Henry.

"Especially when the Huskies are playing — like today."

"Who're we playing today, Henry?"

"Stanford. We'll kill 'em."

"That's good. That's real good." Jill put her tomatoes in a bowl. "Jason, you taking that lettuce out there?"

"Yeah."

"Take these for me, too, will ya?"

"Sure." I took Jill's bowl of tomatoes with my lettuce and went to the salad bar in the front.

Bert was wiping the counter near the cash register. "Hurry up and get that filled, Jason."

"Okay."

I was putting the stuff out on the salad bar when

we got some customers. Two guys came in, a black guy and a white guy. The white guy went in the bathroom and the black guy went up to Bert and started ordering.

"I'll have two hamburgers, two cheeseburgers with everything. Ten fries —"

"Ten orders of fries?"

"Uh-huh, and three Cokes, and two frosties, and the salad bar — and —"

When I heard that, I ran to the back and got the bleu-cheese dressing from the walk-in refrigerator. There are these huge bottles of salad dressing that you dump in the containers on the salad bar. Bert had filled all of them except for the bleu cheese — bleu cheese is very popular. I guess he forgot that. I unscrewed the top of the jar and took the dressing bottle out to the front. When I got back, I couldn't believe it — the guy was still ordering.

"Four orders of chili —"

I dumped the salad dressing in the container. That guy must be starving.

"Oh, God!" Bert yelled.

I looked up and the salad dressing jar I was holding slid right through my hands. Glass shattered and the bleu-cheese dressing flew everywhere.

Standing there with a sawed-off shotgun was the white guy. He had come out of the bathroom and he was standing there and pointing that gun, a real gun, right at Bert!

The black guy turned to me. "You. Get over here."

I just stood there.

He came over to me and picked up one of the chairs with one hand and shoved it in my back. "I said, move, man!" he yelled and shoved the chair in my back again.

I don't know if it hurt, because I felt like I was somebody else, like I had left my body or something and was out there in space watching this guy shove the chair in my back while I got where he wanted me to go, behind the counter next to Bert. We stood there while the other guy pointed the shotgun at us.

Nothing seemed real except the salad dressing. It had splattered on my hat and it dripped down on my face in big blobs.

CHAPTER 3

"WHO peed?"

"What?" Jill whispered.

"Who peed?" Henry hissed again through his teeth.

"Huh?" I whispered to Henry. He and Jill and I were all tied up together in a heap on the floor of the storeroom. Everything was all a blur. All the time the robbers were shoving us and poking us with the gun to make us get down on the storeroom floor while they tied us up, I felt like I was someone else watching. All my senses were screwed up. I heard this rushing sound in my head, sort of like blood going through my brain. I thought I heard the robbers in the office with Bert, making him open the safe, but I couldn't tell for sure with the rushing noise in my head. Then I heard Henry again.

"There." Henry nodded toward the floor. "See?"

"They're gonna kill Bert, then they'll kill us," Jill whispered.

"Which one of you peed?" Henry hissed again.

I looked in the corner. Tipped over on its side was a huge jar of pickles. It must have got knocked over when they shoved us in the storeroom. "It's pickle juice," I whispered to Henry, as the yellow stuff seeped under us.

"What?"

"Pickle juice."

"None of you guys peed?"

I shook my head.

"They're gonna kill us," Jill whispered again. Her hands were tied together behind her back like mine and Henry's, but her fingers were free and I felt them curl around mine. "It's been nice workin' with you, Jason. It's been nice knowing you."

I hadn't stopped feeling numb. The whole thing still seemed like a dream or something, but when I felt Jill's hand holding on to mine, while the rope cut into my wrist, my heart started to pound like crazy. I might die. I might really die. They might shove Bert in here and then shoot us all so there wouldn't be any witnesses. People do stuff like that — *there are rotten people in the world who do stuff like that.*

"I'm scared. Jason, I'm so scared!" Jill's eyes were wide and shiny.

"Me, too," I said, holding on as tight as I could.

"Henry, say something," Jill whispered. "Don't tell me you're not scared."

Henry's hands were tied to my legs. He turned and

25

tried to look at Jill, who was tied up with her arms tied to mine. Henry just nodded.

It seemed to me that I should say *something* if I was going to die — like good-bye or something. I didn't know what to say so I just said what Jill said. "It's been nice knowing you, Jill. Nice knowing you too, Henry."

"Likewise," Henry mumbled.

My hand was really sweaty; Jill's probably was, too. It was hard to tell which sweat belonged to which person the way our hands were stuck together. Then it occurred to me that I could be about to die and that the heaviest relationship I'd ever had with a girl would be right here in this storeroom, huddled up to Jill, holding hands, sitting in pickle juice with Henry Ramos tied to my legs. It was pitiful. But it seemed like what I deserved. If you live like a wimp, you die like a wimp.

I thought I heard them coming out of the office. It could be over, it could be over in just a few minutes. I heard their footsteps. One of those guys must have been wearing boots or something, it sounded like loud thuds — or was that me making the thuds? Like my heart? I listened to that loud pounding noise and it was right then and there that I made myself a promise. "Jason Kovak," I said to myself, "if you get out of this alive you're going to try to quit being a wimp."

As the thuds got louder, I thought about the promise I had just made to myself. Even the promise wasn't very forceful. I didn't say "I'll quit being a wimp!" All I said was "I'll *try* to quit being a wimp." I was thinking about this and getting discouraged about ever moving away from the wimp stance in life when the robbers opened the storeroom door and shoved in Bert. Bert's face was white. Veins stuck out on his neck like a road map. When they shoved him he slid on the wet floor and crashed down on top of Henry's shins.

"Not one a you say nothin'." The white guy stood there pointing the gun at us while the black guy made Bert sit up from where he was lying on the floor. He tied him to Henry. Jill's fingers curled tighter around my hand.

Henry had his head down, he was mumbling. "HailMaryFullofGracetheLordis —"

"I SAID SHUT UP!" The white guy kicked him.

They slammed the storeroom door and I heard it click as they locked it behind them.

"BlessedartThouamongwomenandblessedisthefruit ofThywombJesusHolyMaryMoth . . ." Henry's eyes were closed and his lips were moving but we couldn't hear him too well.

"Prayforussinnersnowandatthehourofourdeatha-menHailMaryFullofGracetheLordis . . ." Henry kept mumbling while the rest of us were quiet.

I looked up at the shelves. There were huge jars of ketchup and mayonnaise and five different kinds of salad dressing. Mayonnaise might be one of the last things in the world I would see. I started counting the jars.

"Who peed?" Jill hissed.

27

"It's pickle juice, remember?" I said.

"Prayforussinnersnowandatthehourofourdeath
. . ."

"That pickle juice was cold, Jason," Jill whispered.
"This is warm!"

I felt something warm seeping under my butt. "Oh
yuk —"

"Shh," Bert said, "I hear something. Maybe
they're back."

"HolyMaryMotherof . . ."

"Shh, Henry." Bert kind of shoved him, but Henry
kept on mumbling.

It was quiet, all except for Henry that is.

Then Jill whispered to me, "It must have been
Bert."

I looked at her and nodded. She was right. Bert
must have peed.

"What?" Bert whispered.

"Nothin'." Jill looked at me and rolled her eyes.

All of us except for Henry listened. It was real
quiet. Then Bert nudged Henry. "Henry, I don't
think you have to pray anymore. I think they're
gone."

We all just sat there. We didn't hear a sound. I
could hear Bert and Henry and Jill breathing. I
didn't know people breathed so loud. I started counting the buns. Not the people's, the hamburgers'. Next
to the ketchup and the mayonnaise and stuff there
were hundreds of huge packages of buns. We waited
like that; it seemed like hours. Just listening and
breathing. I wondered what everyone else was think-

ing about. All I was doing was counting hamburger buns.

Finally, Bert said, "I guess there's no reason for them to come back. They got all the money."

"How do we get out of here?" Jill asked.

Bert twisted his hands around in the rope, then he stopped. "Actually," he said, dropping his hands and taking a deep breath, "I don't *want* to get out of here."

"Are you crazy, man?" Henry had finally stopped praying.

Bert's voice cracked. "I forgot to make the night deposit last night."

Henry whistled through his teeth. "How much they get? Did they get it all? Everything from Friday?"

"All of it — $2739.66. That was the exact amount. I know because I had gotten it all ready for the night deposit and I made out the deposit slip. But I was so tired when I closed up that I just figured I'd do it tonight, with today's receipts."

"Oh, man, you're gonna be in trouble with Gordon." Jill just shook her head.

Gordon Dingerman was the district manager of Wendy's. He was Bert's boss. The store managers, that's what Bert is, are supposed to make the night deposit every night because they're not supposed to leave the money overnight in the safe. It's a rule of the company. Bert was going to be in deep shit. I was thinking about this when we heard someone.

"IS ANYBODY BACK THERE?"

We all just looked at each other.

"HEY — IS ANYBODY BACK THERE?

"I DON'T THINK THERE'S ANYBODY BACK THERE!"

We sat there staring at each other. We couldn't believe it. It was Doris Wainwright, also known by us as Doris the Dingbat. No mistaking that voice. She's this weird old lady who comes in every day and yells, "Where's the beef?" and other stuff like that from the Wendy's commercials. They haven't shown those commercials for years but Doris Wainwright still thinks it's hilarious. Doris also complains about everything and is always threatening to go to McDonald's. We wish she would.

Bert tried to yell. "We're here. We're here!" but he started laughing too hard and you couldn't figure out what he was saying.

"Help! Help!" Jill started yelling and then she cracked up.

"Ha-ha, ha, help! Help!" I tried to yell, too.

The next thing we knew Doris was pounding on the door to the storeroom. "If you don't come out, I'm going to McDonald's!"

"We can't come out," Bert said. "We're locked in here."

"We've been robbed," Henry said.

"Yeah, we've been robbed," Jill said.

"Oh. Shall I unlock the door?"

"That would be very nice of you, Doris," Bert said.

She unlocked the door, opened it, and stood there staring down at us. "Oh," she said, "well, maybe I better go to McDonald's." She turned and started to walk away. I couldn't believe it.

"Doris," Bert called out, "we'd appreciate it, if you could help untie us."

"Oh." She turned around and looked down at us again. "Yes, well, I guess so."

Henry was closest to the door so she untied him first, and as soon as Henry was untied she just left. Incredible. They don't come much dingier than Doris Wainwright.

Henry untied the rest of us and when Bert was free he went and locked the doors of the restaurant and put the CLOSED sign on the door. Then he went back to the office and called the police.

When Bert got off the phone from talking with the police he came into the front of the restaurant to talk to us. "I'm sorry, you guys, but they want everyone to wait here. They want to talk to each one of us."

"I want to go home, Bert." Jill looked down at her pants. "I just want to get out of this place and I want to get out of these stinky clothes." She looked at me. "Don't you want to change too, Jason?"

"Yeah." Besides everything else I'd been sitting in, I still had that salad dressing crap all over my pants. But mostly, I just wanted to get out of there, away from where it had all happened.

"I don't know what to tell you. The police just said they wanted to talk to everyone. They should be here any minute." Bert headed back toward the office. "Well, I guess I gotta do it. Wish me luck, you guys."

"Do what?" Henry sat down at one of the tables near the salad bar.

"Call Gordon."

"Man, I'm glad it's you and not me, that's all I can say." Henry scratched his head.

"Good luck, Bert," Jill said.

"Yeah," I said, as I sat down next to Henry.

The three of us just sat there while we waited for Bert to come back. Outside it had started to rain. It was a light rain, a hazy drizzle, the kind we get a lot of in Seattle. I looked out the window. A car had driven into the parking lot and was heading for the drive-through window. I couldn't believe it. It was Karen Jacobsen with this senior, a big gorilla from the football team, Chip Hornsby. Bert had put the CLOSED sign on the window on his way to the office to call Gordon and in a minute their car headed back out toward the street. While they waited to turn, Chip Hornsby looked back and saw the three of us sitting around the table. The big gorilla gave us the finger and then drove off. I felt terrible. I didn't know if Hornsby was just pissed because he thought we put the CLOSED sign up for the hell of it and we were just sitting around, or if Karen Jacobsen saw me and told him about me finking out on her last night. Everything in my life seemed to be getting worse. It was even raining harder.

"Oh, man." Henry looked out the window as they drove off. He had seen him too.

"I wish the police would get here." Jill tapped the

table with her nails. She had long red fingernails and they went clickity-click on the table. "I gotta get outa these clothes. I can't stand it." She looked down at her hands and she held them out in front of her. "My God, I'm still shaking. Are you, Jason?"

"Yeah." I was, too. I felt like I had a motor running inside me. Just then Bert came back from the office. He looked even whiter than he had when they'd dumped him into the storeroom with us. He slumped down in the chair next to me and sat there with his hands covering his face.

"What happened?" Jill put her hand on his arm.

Bert slumped even further. He just sat there like a bag of potatoes. His face looked all pasty and lumpy — he reminded me of this toy I had when I was a little kid, Mr. Potato Head.

Jill and Henry and I looked at each other. All you could hear was the rain drumming against the windows. Outside, a police car with its front headlights shining came down Mountainview Avenue and turned into the parking lot. It stopped in front of the door on the north side of the building.

Jill saw the policemen and leaned closer to Bert. "What's going on?"

"Gordon thinks I did it."

"What?" Henry's eyes were huge. "Am I hearin' you right, man? Did you just say that Gordon thinks you did it?"

Bert nodded. "He thinks I did it." His voice was so puny we could hardly hear him.

Outside, the policemen had gotten out of their car and were standing at the side door. There were two of them. One guy was black and he was pretty tall; the shorter guy was blond with a moustache. I don't know what it is about policemen, but whenever I see them I feel guilty. It's weird. It doesn't last a long time — I don't wallow around forever in guilt or anything like that, just for a few seconds. As soon as Bert saw them he jumped up and went over to the door and unlocked it. He let them in and then locked the door behind them, still keeping up the CLOSED sign.

The policemen were pretty nice. The tall guy reminded me of this policeman who used to come to visit the kids at John Muir School — I went there for kindergarten until third grade. He was called Officer Friendly. I'm not sure if that was his real name, but that's what he was called. He came to school to talk to us kids, to teach us about safety and how the policeman is our friend.

These officers took down our names and asked each one of us to tell them exactly what we saw and to describe the robbers. Every once in a while, as we were telling them all about it, some cars would drive in the parking lot and see the CLOSED sign and the police car and then leave. No one in the cars seemed to mind that the place was closed when they saw the police inside with us. Well, maybe they did mind, but at least no one else gave us the finger. We were showing the policemen the storeroom when we heard the door being unlocked.

"All right. Where is he?"

It's usually hard for Gordon Dingerman to move very fast. He's a fat guy with a big beer belly. He has a walrus moustache — in fact, his whole face looks like a walrus and he's bald except for one long piece of black hair, which he combs over the top of his head. It's supposed to cover his baldness. If he only knew.

"Well, did you arrest him?"

"Who are you?" The policeman who looked like Officer Friendly stared at Gordon.

Gordon stuck out a big beefy paw. "Gordon Dingerman. District manager for Wendy's." His hand pumped up and down as he shook hands with Officer Friendly. "I'm their boss," he said, waving his other hand in our direction, "and this man," he pointed a fat finger at Bert, "this man left the money in the safe! If that doesn't show he's involved in this robbery, I don't know what does!"

"Mr. Dongerman." The policeman's voice was firm.

"Dingerman."

"Yes, uh, Mr. Dingerman, all it shows is that he left money in the safe."

"You're not going to arrest him?"

"No."

"Could we talk to you a minute — in private?" Jill looked up at the Officer Friendly guy.

"Sure."

I wasn't sure who Jill meant by "we," but I was hoping it didn't include me. I just wanted to get this

35

whole thing over with and get out of there as fast as I could.

"Come on, Jason," she said.

I shrugged my shoulders and looked around and then, true to form, instead of saying anything I just followed her back to the office. After we got in there she closed the door.

"I just wanted to tell you, Officer, that Jason and I know that Bert didn't do it."

I *really* wanted to get out of there when Jill said that. I had an awful feeling I knew what was coming.

"All right. Do you want to tell me about it?" He looked at me and then he looked at Jill.

Jill looked at me and then looked at the policeman and whispered, "It's because Bert peed."

"What?"

"See, we didn't know who it was at first, because at first when Henry said someone peed, it was pickle juice, but then after Bert was thrown in there — it was warm!"

"Warm?" The policeman looked at Jill like she had cracked under the stress. I wanted to crawl through the floor.

"Right. It was warm, and that's how we knew it was Bert who peed."

The policeman stared at us.

"Because he was so scared. Don't you see? He peed on the floor because he was so scared, and if he had been the robber he wouldn't have been scared like that. Right, Jason?"

I couldn't believe I was part of this brilliant detective work. "Yeah," I mumbled.

"I see. Well thank you for this, uh, information and I will, uh, keep it in mind."

"See — we didn't want to tell you in front of Bert and Henry 'cause it might embarrass him."

"Yes, I can see that."

We were quiet as we left the office and walked back to join the others. I was wondering if my book *5000 One and Two Liners for Any and Every Occasion* had anything in it to fit this situation. I couldn't believe Jill told that officer about Bert peeing on the floor like it was big evidence and that I just stood there like I thought so, too.

Henry and Bert were sitting at a table and the other policeman was standing at the counter, filling out a report.

"Did Gordon leave?" Jill asked as she and I sat down next to Bert and Henry.

"He drove to the main office to get some money for the cash register — so we can open. He'll be right back."

The policeman came over and told us that if they caught the suspects they'd be notifying us to come downtown to see if we could identify them. I wanted them to catch the robbers, but I have to admit that the idea of having to point them out in a lineup, having to put the finger, as they say, on a vicious, hardened criminal, would not exactly be my idea of a good time.

After the policemen told us that we'd hear from them if they caught the guys, they checked over the forms they had filled out to make sure they had all our names and addresses and our home phone numbers. Then they headed toward the door. Bert unlocked it and let them out.

As the police car drove away, Bert leaned back against the door and sighed. "Well, I guess I'll be seein' you guys." Then he stood up and walked slowly back to the office. When he came back he was wearing his jacket.

"Where are you going, man?" Henry asked.

"Home, I guess. Gordon fired me."

"When did he do that?" Jill just shook her head.

"On the phone when I called him. First he said I was fired, then he said to stay here until the police came so they could arrest me."

"So we're supposed to work with Gordon as manager when he gets back?" Henry asked.

"Yeah, I guess so."

"Not me." Jill stood up. "That tub of lard comes in here, tells the cops to arrest you, and never once asks how we are! Never says he feels bad about what we went through! No way will I work for him. He can take this job and shove it."

"I'm going to McDonald's," Henry said. "How 'bout you, Jason, you gonna quit too?"

"Yeah." I looked at Henry and Jill and I blurted out, "Me, too," not really sure if I was just following along as usual or taking a stand on something for the first time in my life.

Jill ripped a napkin from the napkin holder. She wrote a note and we all signed our names and left it on the table so Gordon would see it when he came back. Then we walked out, locking the door behind us. The note said:

Dear Gordon,

    WE QUIT.

Sincerely,
    Jill Washington
    Henry Ramos
    Jason Kovak

CHAPTER 4

IT was weird trying to say good-bye to Jill and Henry at the bus stop. Henry wanted all of us to march right down the street to McDonald's and ask for jobs, but Jill said all she wanted to do was go home and take a bath. That's what I wanted to do, too (not go home with Jill to take a bath, I mean — although, come to think of it, that's a fantastic thought). I certainly wasn't about to go apply for a job at McDonald's looking like this. But I knew how Henry felt, wanting us to stick together and all. At the bus stop we started saying good-bye, but we just kept hanging around. We kept talking about the robbery, about how scared we were and thinking we would be killed, and the funny stuff, too. Henry said those robbers were the Ebony and Ivory of crime, and we laughed and then cracked up all over again about Doris Wainwright saying, "I don't think there's anybody back there!" We kept talking about what had happened over and over again — no one wanted to leave. War buddies probably feel like that. Henry even missed his bus and had to wait for the next one.

After we finally split up, I walked home. Instead of going into the house, I walked right on by. You can see the lake from our back yard. I walked by the house, and headed down the steps that lead to the lake. It was still raining, but just a real light rain. Lake Washington was so gray you could hardly see the other side. I crossed Lake Washington Boulevard and the jogging and bike trail and went down the bank toward the water. Not too many leaves were left on the trees; we'd had a big windstorm last week. It always makes me sad when most of the branches are bare. Especially when all the leaves have been all golden and so pretty and everything and then they just float away and there's nothing left. I wasn't sure why I was sitting there in the rain. That happens to me sometimes, I just do stuff.

I broke apart some sticks that were on the ground. They snapped even though they were wet.

I couldn't help thinking about that promise I made myself when I thought they were going to kill me — that I would try not to be a wimp anymore. Had I begun not to be one when I quit Wendy's with Jill and Henry? It was weird, but I didn't even know. Quitting with them felt good, but maybe I was just going along with stuff like I usually do. No big deal. Jill and Henry quit, so I did what they did. Nothin' new, I guess. But somehow it did feel different.

I took a big stick and broke it in half. Up on the jogging trail, I noticed Mrs. Weber, my friend Chris's mother, going by. She didn't see me. I didn't wave or anything, I just scrunched down by the tree and looked out at the lake. I broke some more sticks. It's not right about mothers. They don't look like mothers anymore. Mothers should look like the Pillsbury Doughboy — kind of plump and pillowy and floury soft. Most mothers these days are bony like my mom. Very bony. They look my age jumping around in little skimpy clothes to Jane Fonda records and jogging around in little shorts, looking sexy. It's not right.

When Mrs. Weber had jogged out of sight, I got up and headed back across the boulevard and up the steps to 34th Avenue. It was still raining and I was getting cold. A car passed me as I was walking down the block toward my house. It honked and backed up and stopped right next to me. It was a Corvette — my dad's car. He bought a bright red Corvette after mom moved out. Typical, right? She leaves and he does this bachelor number toolin' around town in his red 'Vette. That's what he calls it, too, his 'Vette. Sad, but true. My dad is right out of the fifties. He got stuck in 1955.

"Jason!" he yelled at me. "You on your way home?"

"Yeah."

"Gonna be there long?"

"Dunno."

"Yeah, well see ya, Jason."

He roared off down the street. I know kids who drive slower than he does.

I'm not dumb. I know the reason he asks how long I'm going to be home is so he can find out whether he'll have the house all to himself with that lady. I hardly looked at this one except to notice that she was blond. Most of the women he goes out with are blond. My mother is blond. Her hair is all shiny and kind of golden and pretty. There's something golden about all of her — it's hard to explain.

When I got inside I went straight down to the basement and pulled off my clothes. The next thing I did was get in the shower. The warm water felt good. But as I started feeling warmer and relaxed, my back started to hurt like hell. Maybe I hadn't noticed it before because I had been so cold, or maybe I had been cold and numb from fright. I reached around and felt this big swollen place. Some of the skin had broken and when I looked at my hands there was blood on them. All of a sudden I felt weak. I crumpled up and just sat in the bottom of the shower. I looked at my hands again and there were red swollen marks where the ropes had cut across my wrists. It was weird. I hadn't even known that stuff was there.

I sat in the bottom of the shower for a while longer and closed my eyes. My head was tilted up toward the shower head and I just let the water run down my face. I thought about the robbery. I could see the way the whole thing should have gone.

The minute I see the guy with the sawed-off shot-

43

gun, like lightning, I heave the jar of salad dressing. My arm is like a gun, better than Fouts, better than Marino, better than Elway, better than Montana. The salad dressing hits the creep in the face, the glass splatters, it cuts him a little — just a little, on his nose. His gun is covered with bleu cheese, but he tries to fire anyway, as his fellow robber comes toward me. But always quick and brave (I'm known as Jason, the Quick and the Brave) I start heaving another jar of dressing. WHAP! French dressing gets him in the crotch. BAM! The oil and vinegar knocks his buddy in the kneecaps. SPLAT! Green Goddess to the groin. I jump across the room and tie them up with their own ropes. Then I dump all the lettuce and vegetables on their heads. "Just a little something to go with the salad dressing, boys," I say in a deep voice. Everyone laughs (except the robbers). Jill and I go home and take a bath together.

Finally, I stood up and washed my hair. When I got out of the shower, I put a towel around my waist and picked up the Wendy's outfit and took it back to the washing machine and threw it in. It would be strange not going there anymore. One thing was good though, we had just gotten paid Friday, the day before, so if Gordon Dingerman got stingy and behaved like the scumbag we all know he is, we really wouldn't be out that much money for the time we were there Saturday. Why should we lose any money though? Maybe we could tell him we wouldn't give his lousy uniforms back unless he paid us for the morning. Sort of like blackmail. "No money . . . no uniform, Dingerman," I said, practicing my deep voice.

"Jason!" Dad yelled down the basement stairs.

"Yeah."

"Are you leaving for work pretty soon?"

"Nope." I wondered if I should tell him. I didn't wonder long though. I don't know what happened. All of a sudden I just yelled at the top of my lungs. "I QUIIIIIIT!"

"What?" My dad yelled down the stairs.

"I QUIT!" I turned on the washing machine and walked back to my room and started getting dressed.

"Francine, this will just take me a minute, honey," I could hear Dad say. Then he came down to my room. This was a grand occasion. A very big deal. As I mentioned, my dad never comes down to my room.

"Did I hear you right, Jason? What d'ya mean you quit?" He looked around the room. "God, this place is a mess!"

"Yeah."

"Yeah what? Yeah, you quit? Or yeah, this place is a mess?" He was beginning to sound real irritated now.

"Both."

"What's wrong with you, anyway? Jobs are hard to get. You can't just up and quit a perfectly good job. Don't you care about college? You know our deal — I'll pay the tuition —"

"I know. I pay room and board."

"Well, if you know that, Jason —" Dad looked at the big flashy gold watch on his hairy arm. Sometimes I've wondered how come he's so hairy and I'm not. "Listen, I've got to go. This is not the end of this, Jason. I want to hear why you just up and quit a perfectly good job. Jobs are hard to find, you know."

I nodded. (You already said that.)

"We're going to talk about this." He turned and went back up the stairs. After he left, I wished I had told him about the robbery. I had wanted to, but when a person starts a conversation with, "What's wrong with you, anyway?" you don't exactly feel like spilling your guts. I always clam up when Dad comes on like that. Besides, he was in such a hurry to leave with that lady, it didn't seem like the right time. I suppose Dad was worried that he'd have to support me for the rest of his life and that he'd be stuck with me living there forever, putting a damper on his action. (I wish *I* had some action.)

I got the *Weekly* out from under my bed and started reading the personal column again. Right in between

> TAKE MY HAND! Let's feel the magic. Dark-eyed beauty, classy and sharp, seeks devilish gentle male. Age not important. Box 66933, Seattle, WA 98112

and

> ATTRACTIVE BISEXUAL FEMALE seeks same. Box 17572, Seattle, WA 98105

was one that caught my eye. It looked like it was in the wrong column.

HELP WANTED. Consultant desired for position of importance. Send your philosophy of life to PO Box 9663, Seattle, WA 98144

I sat and stared at it. What *was* my philosophy of life anyway? Only a few hours before I'd sat counting large mayonnaise jars and hamburger buns, convinced I was about to die, and all I could think about was not wanting to be a wimp. If I have a philosophy of life it must be more than that. I went to my desk to look for my dictionary. My desk was piled with those books that were supposed to prepare me for my career with women. The pile was growing even though my career wasn't (I had recently found *The Sensuous Man* to add to my collection). There was also a pile of *The Adventures of Tintin.* Kenny Newman and I always used to get off on the fact that Tintin books are printed in thirty-one different languages and are world famous. While we were hanging out in the Kovak Kan we would imagine some guy reading the exact stuff we read, but in Finnish or Bengali or something. I still get off on that, as a matter of fact.

I finally found my dictionary under *Tintin in Tibet* and looked up the definition of philosophy. It said, "study of the principles underlying conduct, thought, and the nature of the universe, general principles of a field of knowledge, a particular system of ethics."

I got out a piece of paper and tried to figure out the Jason Kovak system of ethics. Finally, I wrote down:

People should be nice to each other.
There should be no bombs.

A person should try to laugh some every day.
Even if there isn't a big laugh every day,
a little one is better than none.
That's about it.

Jason Kovak

After I signed my name, I checked the ad again to
see where to send my philosophy of life. It said PO
Box 9663. As I looked more closely I noticed that a lot
of the ads in the *Weekly* had box numbers. Maybe my
reply would seem more official if I had one, too. I decided to call the post office to find out about boxes.

I was put on hold and there wasn't even music; although mostly when you're on hold the music is
crappy. But finally this guy answered and I found out
it cost eleven dollars to rent a box for six months. I
thought about this for a while. Then I thought, what
the hell? Eleven dollars and a stamp would be the
most I had to lose. And it would be worth it, because
now when Dad hassled me about getting a new job,
as I knew he would, I could tell him I had already
applied for one. Renting the box would make the
whole thing official.

I picked up the *Weekly* again and my eyes, like a
couple of magnets, got stuck on the ad:

> TAKE MY HAND! Let's feel the magic.
> Dark-eyed beauty, classy and sharp, seeks
> devilish gentle male. Age not important. Box
> 66933, Seattle, WA 98112.

I had just answered the Help Wanted ad, why
couldn't I answer this one, too? I had imagined doing

it enough times, that's for sure. I mean every time I read the ads, I imagined answering one. And this one said, "Age not important." I mean, it said that — right there in black and white — AGE NOT IM-PORTANT — I just stared at it over and over. What the hell? What did I have to lose anyway? Another stamp. Big deal. (Oh my God.) I got a piece of paper out of my desk and I began to write, just like I had imagined it at least a hundred times.

> *Dear Dark-eyed Beauty,*
>
> *I was impressed with the fine spirit of adventure you indicated by placing your enticing ad in the personal column of the* Weekly. *I am a citizen of New Zealand and have recently returned from Tibet, where I climbed Mt. Everest, which in Tibetan is called Chomolungma. I am in Seattle to pick up my yacht which was being repaired here while I was in Tibet and I'll be sailing for New Zealand in about a month. I am a devilish, gentle male and would enjoy making your acquaintance during my layover in the Pacific Northwest. I can be reached through PO Box   Seattle, WA 98144.*
>
> > *Yours very truly,*
> > *T. Worthington Jones*

I left the box number blank. I decided I would fill it in and also put down the box number on my reply to the help-wanted ad after I went to the post office to rent the box. I was especially glad I had decided to rent a box because I didn't want any mail coming to the house addressed to T. Worthington Jones. Even

49

though I had been familiar with T. Worthington Jones for many years, Dad (and everyone else in the world, for that matter) didn't know he existed, and I preferred to keep it that way. T. Worthington Jones was the name I called myself when I imagined having fantastic adventures like Tintin. When I was younger, T. Worthington charged around the world capturing international criminals. Lately, he's been heavily into women. Zillions of them. They love him. They're all over him. Not just because he's so rich, either. He's quite a fascinating guy.

I decided to type the letter because my writing wasn't so hot. Mom had taken the typewriter when she moved out, so after I went to the post office I'd have to go over to her place to use it.

I wondered if I was flipping out. Maybe I had just now gone totally nuts. It's Loony Tune Time at Jason's house, folks. But then I said to myself, What the hell? What do I have to lose? The price of a box and two stamps. Big deal. (Oh my God.)

I went to the post office.

CHAPTER 5

"JASON, you really should call before you come over."

Mom stood in the doorway of her houseboat. She was all dressed up. It seemed like a pretty fancy dress for a Saturday afternoon.

"Who is it, Marlene?"

"It's Jason," she called over her shoulder to Roger Albright, commonly referred to as "That Fruitcake" by my dad, as I mentioned.

"Oh, yes. Hello, Jason," he said.

"Hi."

"Well, come on in, Jason, but we'll just be here for a short time." Mom kissed my cheek. Her perfume smells like vanilla extract. I like how it smells but as I said before she does not look like the Pillsbury Doughboy — the cooking thing with my mother starts and stops these days with the perfume smell.

"Roger and I are going out to dinner and then we have tickets for the Rep tonight."

Roger Albright, tall, thin, in his tweedy coat with the leather elbow patches, came out of the kitchen and put his arm around Mom. "You're welcome to come over here and see us, Jason. But like your mother said, you should give us a call first, to make sure it's convenient."

It really pissed me off when I heard the word "convenient." I should call to make sure it's *convenient* to see my own mother?

"Yeah, well, I just wanted to use the typewriter."

"Oh, do you have to type something for school, Jason?"

"Yeah."

Lying is not my favorite thing; in fact, I always feel pretty guilty about it. It's not that I go around lying through my teeth all the time or anything like that. But there are times when it is more "convenient" to lie a little.

"It's upstairs, honey." Mom motioned toward the stairs. "Help yourself." Their houseboat has stairs leading up to a loft-type thing which is all one room, a combination bedroom and den. Skylights and stained glass windows are all over the place. Everything about my mother's houseboat is cool. It could be in some magazine, like *Sunset*. In fact, everything about Mom and Roger Albright is like that, like it came out of some magazine. Their food, for instance — they eat stuff like goat-cheese pizza with calamata olives and stuffed grape leaves, and Roger

Albright has this Rolex watch and drives a BMW, of course. I sat down in the den part of the room where the typewriter was. It was at a built-in desk. Roger Albright is an architect and Mom is an interior designer — they have built-in stuff all over the place. This desk was built in front of a window that looks out onto Lake Union. Outside it was still raining. The wind blew the drops across the window in big streaks. On the lake, right in front of the houseboat, a family of ducks went swimming by. It was nice — a mom and a dad. You could tell the dad from the mom because of its green head. And two babies.

"Jason?" Mom called up the stairs.

"Yeah?"

"Did you find the typewriter?"

"Yeah."

"Well, Roger and I do have to leave soon."

I reached for a piece of typing paper and put it in the machine. "This'll just take a minute," I yelled down over the edge of the loft.

The piece of paper where I had written my letter to the dark-eyed beauty was kind of crumpled when I took it out of my back pocket. I straightened it out and put it next to the typewriter and started typing. Mom's typewriter was really nice. I wished she had left it at home. Before I started typing I looked out the window again at the family of ducks . . . Not just the typewriter, why couldn't she have left herself at home, too?

But I quit thinking about that and started typing. It didn't take me very long to finish it. I typed the address on the envelope, folded the letter and stuck it in.

On my mother's dresser, also built-in, I noticed a color photo of her and Roger Albright. It was spring and they were standing in the woods. Mom was holding a bunch of wild flowers. Roger had his arm around her shoulder and his sweater was folded over his back with the arms tied over his shoulders, very preppie. I wondered when the picture had been taken. I looked around the room. It's huge. They have a waterbed, built-in, of course. You'd think living on a houseboat they'd get enough of water.

As I went down the stairs from the loft I thought about telling Mom that I almost got killed today in a robbery and that I also quit Wendy's. Probably she'd say that she was sure I was grown-up enough to have handled the whole thing just fine.

"Did you get your work finished, Jason?" Mom was sitting on a white couch in front of a huge window that opens onto a deck. She was sipping champagne. She and the Fruitcake do that a lot, sit around and sip champagne.

"Yeah."

She put her glass down on the chrome table. "Well, Jason. I'm sorry we're on our way out soon. But you really should —"

"I know — call before I come."

Roger Albright held the door open for me. "That's right, just give us a call anytime."

Mom kissed me good-bye and I walked along the dock from their houseboat to the lot where I had parked my car. Dad got me a car after he bought his car because he didn't want me driving his new 'Vette. The car he got me is a ten-year-old Ford: black and cheap. It's not that great on gas so I don't drive it to school, and I always walk to work because Wendy's isn't that far from my house. It's beat up, but it runs. I had parked it next to the Fruitcake's BMW: blue, new, and shiny. Perfect, of course. I had an impulse to bash into it and mess it up a bit. Not demolish it, just a few crunches, like if I was driving a bumper car kiddie ride at Seattle Center. I'd drive around and bump it and go "Wheee!" with each little bump.

I pulled up in front of a mailbox on the way home, hopped out, and mailed both letters before I could change my mind. Would I ever hear from the dark-eyed beauty? Would I actually get a letter back? All the way home I kept thinking about it.

It would be wonderful. There I would be, striding into a dimly lit cocktail lounge with long, purposeful strides. I would hesitate a bit by the bar as my eyes scanned the room. In the corner a woman would lift her eyes to mine. Expectantly, she'd cock her head, looking quizzically at me with deep dark eyes. I would nod to her and cross the room with long, purposeful strides. "You must be T. Worthington Jones," she would say.

"Yes, it is I. And you are . . ."

"Pamela."

"What a beautiful name. It fits you perfectly," I would say, sitting across from her and letting her gaze meet mine.

"You are so young, T. Worthington."

"Yes, I am."

"I had hoped you would be," she'd say with a smoldering look. "I have longed for a young man."

"Pamela?"

"Yes, T. Worthington?"

"Let us not waste this precious time with idle chatter. Wanna do it?"

"Oh yes, yes, yes," she'd say, breathlessly.

When I got home I saw that Dad's car was parked in the driveway. I parked my car on the street because he'd probably be going out again and he always gets mad if I park behind him and block the Corvette.

It was starting to get dark when I walked across the lawn to the house. In the kitchen, I opened the refrigerator and surveyed its bountiful contents, three cans of beer, some orange juice, moldy cheese, half a loaf of rye bread, and a box of Kentucky Fried Chicken with one piece of chicken left in it. I was munching on the chicken when Dad came into the kitchen.

"Sit down, Jason," he said, taking a can of beer out of the refrigerator. "I want to talk to you."

I threw the chicken bone in the garbage and sat down at the table. Dad sat across from me, took a big swig of his beer, and then set the can down.

"Now what's this about you quitting your job?"

"We got robbed."

"You got robbed? Today? At Wendy's?"

"Yeah."

"Anybody get hurt?"

"Not really. I mean, not bad or anything. We just got pushed around and tied up and stuff."

Dad took another sip of his beer. He was real quiet, like he was thinking things over.

"They had a gun."

"A gun?"

"Yeah, a sawed-off shotgun."

"That sounds pretty rough, Jason."

"Yeah."

"Anybody else quit?"

"Yeah. Two other people — Henry and Jill. And the manager, Bert — he got fired."

"How come?"

"He forgot to make the night deposit and the district manager fired him."

"So you all quit because you felt loyal to this Bert, the guy that got fired?"

"Well, sort of, and the district manager, Gordon Dingerman, is a jerk. He didn't say one word about what we'd been through."

"There's a lot of jerks in this world, Jason. And a lot of times you get stuck with a guy for a boss that's a jerk."

"Yeah."

"Now listen, Jason. What happened today sounds like it was pretty rough, but you can't let it get to you. The only person who can decide you've been whipped is you. You've got to get right back out there and get another job."

"Yeah, I guess so." I thought of telling him about the job I had applied for, but it seemed stupid — so I just shut up.

"Look, Jason, I don't expect to support you for the rest of my life. I've got my own life to live, you know."

"Yeah." (As if I hadn't noticed this.)

Dad reached into his pocket and took out his wallet. He pulled out one of his business cards and put it on the table in front of me.

"You see this card here?"

"Yeah." (I'd only seen it about a hundred times.)

"Well this card used to embarrass your mother, but she wasn't too embarrassed spending the money I make, I'll tell you that. This card," he jabbed his finger at it, "this card here represents going for it, Jason. Going for it. And that's what you've gotta do now. You've got to get out there and go for it."

On my father's business cards it says, "Kovak's Kans," in big letters and then there's a picture of him, and under the picture it says, "Jack Kovak, Colonel of the Urinal." It really says that. Can you believe it?

"A lotta people might think that 'Colonel of the Urinal' is a silly little slogan, Jason. But I'll tell you — they never forget it. Nope, they never forget the Colonel and that's proven. I outsell Johnny-on-the-Spot and Sanikans two to one."

I nodded. (I had heard this before — since I was born, to be specific.)

"And you know what, Jason? It all changed when I

decided to go for it. I went to a motivation seminar at the Northwest Institute and I learned to believe in myself. To go for it. And that's when I came up with the slogan. It came to me, during one of the motivation training sessions. It just popped into my head, 'Colonel of the Urinal.' There it was, right in my head, just waiting for me to make money with it. And right after that, as soon as I put it on my business cards and started using the slogan, Kovak's Kans took off like nobody's business. I say my affirmations every morning, Jason. And I want you to start doing it, too."

"Affirmations?"

"Yes. That's what they're called. Every morning, right after I shave, I look at myself in the mirror, right in the eye, and I say, 'I am capable and competent. I am a winner. Today I will be all that I can be.' "

The way he said it, it sounded like a prayer or something. I didn't know my dad was in the bathroom talking to himself in the mirror every morning. Things were getting too weird.

"Say it after me, Jason."

"What?"

"Say it."

"Say what?"

"Say the affirmation. Come on. I am capable."

"I am capable," I sort of whispered.

"And competent."

"Dad, I really don't think I want to do this."

Dad took a big swig of his beer. "All right, Jason. Suit yourself. But try it in front of the mirror. It works. It'll motivate you to go for it. To get right out there and get another job." Dad stood up and threw his beer can in the garbage. "I'm going out tonight, Jason. And I might be staying over at Francine's place. I'll see you sometime tomorrow."

"Okay."

"Those fast-food places are all open on Sunday, Jason. Don't waste any time. Get right out there tomorrow and get yourself a new job. Remember, you can be a winner. Go for it!"

"Yeah."

After Dad left, I went down to my room and called Kenny to see if he wanted to do anything that night. He probably had plans with Stephanie, but I thought I'd try anyway.

"Hi, Kenny."

"How's it going, Jason?"

"I should never have gone to work today — should've gone to the Huskies game with you."

"What happened?"

"We got robbed at Wendy's."

"No shit."

"Yeah, really. It was freaky."

"Anybody get hurt? They get a lot of money?"

"We didn't get hurt, but they got over two grand."

"Man, you must not be too excited about goin' back there to work."

"I'm not. We all quit — Henry Ramos, Jill Washington, and me. Now Dad's hassling me about getting another job. I gotta get out of here. You want to do something tonight?"

"Sure. Stephanie is still with her uncle."

"Great."

"Let's go up to the Ave."

"Okay."

"I'll pick you up in about twenty minutes."

"Okay."

While I was waiting for Kenny to pick me up, for some stupid reason I went in the bathroom and I looked at myself in the mirror, right in the eye.

"I am c-c-capable and c-competent —" I just stood there a minute looking at myself and all I saw was me, Jason Kovak, the wimp. "I am a winner," I said, anyway. "Today I will be all that I can be —"

I stood there looking at myself.

"Oh, crap."

CHAPTER 6

THAT night I woke up about three in the morning with this dream. Actually, it wasn't a dream at all — it was a nightmare. I was all sweaty and the covers were a mess. I'd probably been thrashing around, although I didn't remember doing that. But in it, in the dream — nightmare, I mean — I had been drowning in salad dressing and there were some people with guns shooting lettuce heads and tomatoes were splattered all over and it was all red and slimy from the tomatoes but then it turned into blood. God, it was awful. Then, as soon as I was awake, I thought I started hearing things in the house, this creaking noise — noises, like someone was breaking in.

"Calm yourself, Jason," I told myself in this strong voice.

"Oh shit, I'm scared," I said.

"You just had a bad dream, it's nothing."

"What if it's a robber!"

"Don't be a wimp. It's probably just the furnace or something."

"Or something? Oh my God!"

"Look, just go upstairs and check it out."

"Yeah and come face-to-face with a sawed-off shotgun!"

"Then get a weapon."

"What weapon!"

It went on like this, me talking to myself back and forth like a lunatic. Meanwhile, I was lying there totally frozen stiff, like I was dead.

I couldn't move — it seemed like hours. Finally, I remembered the weight set. I crawled to the end of the bed. Sweat was pouring off my body. I reached down and grabbed the bar. I went over to the door holding the metal bar in my hand like a club and I crept out, shaking a lot. I got as far as the bottom of the basement stairs. I listened there. Everything was real quiet. I just waited, shaking and listening.

"Just go up the goddamn stairs," I told myself.

"Maybe I could run into the bathroom and lock the door and climb out the window."

"Oh great, and run around the neighborhood in your underpants at three in the morning waving the bar from your weight set."

So I put one foot on the stairs, then another. It was agony. Slowly I climbed them. I listened at each step. And when I didn't hear anything, I'd go up one more step. When I got up to the kitchen, I held the bar over my head with one hand while I switched on the light with the other.

The kitchen was empty. Everything was quiet. So I went from room to room like that. Slowly, through the whole goddamn house, putting the lights on in every room. Upstairs, my dad's room was the last place I had to look. I put one hand on the doorknob and I had the bar over my head. But I froze again.

"Open the door, dummy."

"I'm scared."

"Just do it."

"What if he's in there?"

"You would have heard him."

"But he could be in there!"

"Go in and bash him!"

"Oh, crap."

"Do it! You've come this far."

"Oh what the hell." I held the bar over my head, whipped open the door and switched on the light.

Empty. It was totally empty. For a minute I got panicky. What had happened to Dad? But then I remembered that he was over at the lady's house, whatever her name was — Francine, that was it. He was with Francine, probably having a major-league good time. Big Jack Kovak the Toilet King in the Superbowl of Sex. Capable and competent. Go for it!

Crap.

I saw his golf bag propped up in the corner of the room. So I took the metal bar and I went over to his clubs and just smashed hell out of the bag. I pretended it was a robber or something. Bam! Take that, you dirtbag! Whap! — and that, you scum!

Then I went back down to the kitchen and got a beer out of the refrigerator and took it down to my room. I left the lights on everywhere in the whole house. It seemed like a good idea. If there were any robbers out there they'd think there were a whole lot of people home. In my room, I sat up in bed and drank the beer. I kind of chugged it. Then I went up to the kitchen and got another one and chugged that, too. Then I felt sick. I'll bet it was five in the morning before I got back to sleep.

It was noon when I finally woke up. When I got up the first thing I did was to go and look in the garage. No Corvette. He still wasn't back. I scrounged around the kitchen. There wasn't anything good in the refrigerator and I didn't feel like sitting around reading the back of the Wheaties box while I ate cold cereal so I decided to go to McDonald's to get an Egg McMuffin.

As I pulled out of the driveway I noticed that I was pretty low on gas. That was something else I supposed I would have to start worrying about, seeing as I have to pay for my own gas.

When I went in there were just three people in front of me. A man and a lady and their little kid. I guess I was staring at them. It was kind of embarrassing, staring like that, but the little kid — it was a girl — had on a little dress, and the parents were dressed up too, like they had come from church or something. The mom was holding the little kid's hand and it was real nice. It just got me it was so nice.

I was staring at them so much that I didn't even notice until it was my turn to order that Henry Ramos was the guy on the register taking the orders.

"Hey, Jason."

"Hi." I was real glad to see Henry. He sure hadn't wasted any time getting another job.

"How's it going, man?" Henry grinned.

"Okay, I guess."

"They got a camera here. See?" Henry pointed to this camera up over the cash register.

"That's good."

"Keeps the crooks away."

"Uh-huh."

"It's a lot better'n Wendy's."

"Yeah."

"I been workin' here since yesterday. I just marched down here after the robbery and got myself a job."

"Yeah, just like you said you would."

"Yeah. What'll ya have, man?"

"An Egg McMuffin."

"Anything else?"

"Oh milk, I guess, and maybe some fries."

"We got hashbrowns."

"Okay, hashbrowns."

"That'll be it?"

"Yeah. Uh, say, Henry, uh — they need anybody else here?"

"Nope. Don't think so."

"Do you have an application around anyway? Uh, maybe I could just fill one out."

"Sure, no problem." Henry got me an application from the office and then handed it to me with the milk I had ordered. "I'll put a good word in for you, man."

"Thanks, Henry."

When my order was up I took it to a table in the back. The hashbrowns were pretty good. After I finished eating, I filled out the application. While I was filling it out, I watched Henry. He seemed pretty happy back there in his McDonald's outfit taking orders and talking to the people. I remembered how he'd been praying when we were tied up. Henry sure had bounced back fast. I don't think he had to look at himself in the mirror and say a bunch of crap, either. He just went out there and did it.

After I left McDonald's I went to Burger King. Same thing — they didn't need anybody, but I filled out an application anyway. Drove down to Taco Time — didn't need anybody, but I filled out an application. Hit Kentucky Fried Chicken on the way home — didn't need anybody but I filled out an application. Everywhere I went they said they didn't need anybody.

The whole dumb week went like that. Meanwhile I was getting lower and lower on gas. It was terrible at school, too, because I had to figure out ways to avoid Karen Jacobsen. After screwing up our date, facing her was the last thing I wanted to do. I had two plans for avoiding her: the sleep plan and the bathroom plan. Every morning in homeroom, I pretended to be asleep while I barricaded myself behind my French book. Then, during the day, whenever I saw her bouncing down the hall, I flew into the john. It was wearing me out, always having to be on the lookout for her. (I also got tired of spending so much time in the john.)

On Wednesday after second period, I practically had my whole head in my locker, scrounging around trying to find my geometry book, when I felt a tap on my shoulder.

"Jason?"

I jumped back and banged my head against the door of the locker. It was Karen!

"Oh, I didn't mean to scare you." She giggled.

"Um — I, uh — didn't see you."

"Well, I just wondered if you were okay. You've been asleep every morning in homeroom. I hope you got over the flu."

"Yeah."

"Well, see you later." She smiled and went bouncing down the hall.

After she left, I watched her walk away. Then I stood looking in my locker, wishing I could have said something besides "yeah." I thought of how I wished things had gone. That always happens, I always think of stuff after the person leaves.

After she tapped me on the shoulder, I would turn slowly, and gaze down at her. "Karen," I'd say in a deep voice.

"Oh, Jason, I've been so worried about you."

"Nothing to worry about, gorgeous. I'm well and strong now." Then I'd scoop her up in my arms. "See!"

I banged the locker door shut and left for geometry. On the way to class, I decided to quit both plans for avoiding her. At least she was still speaking to me, even if I couldn't think of anything to say back.

Things went a little better after I made that decision. It was good not to have to spend so much time in the john. But that night I dreaded going home, and every night that week for that matter, because Dad was hassling me more every day.

On Monday, as soon as he got home from work, the first thing he said was, "Got a new job yet, Jason?" (Not even "Hello.") On Tuesday he said, "I know job hunting's hard, Jason, but you've got to get out there and pound the pavement." This was followed again by his half-hour speech on what the Northwest Institute had done for him, how his business took off after he became Colonel of the Urinal, and it ended up with his telling me how he outsells Johnny-on-the-Spot and Sanikan, two to one — blah blah blah. I think I could give this speech myself, I've heard it so often. On Wednesday he said, "Don't you realize you've got to get a job — that is, if you want to go to college, Jason." Thursday night he said, "Jason, do you understand the consequences of not working? I am not going to support you for the rest of my life." On Friday, I was down in my room reading the *Weekly* when he yelled down the stairs to me.

"Jason!"

"Yeah."

"Come up here!"

Dad was in the kitchen with the freezer door open. We had a whole bunch of frozen dinners in there.

"Which one of these do you want?"

"Stouffer's lasagna, I guess."

"It's still pretty early, do you want to eat now?"

"Yeah, I guess so."

"Okay, I'll put mine in now too. I didn't get a break for lunch today, so I came home early. I'm ready to eat." He took the lasagna package out of the freezer along with one for himself and went over to the microwave and popped them in. "Got a job yet, Jason?"

"Nope."

"You know you can't afford to fool around like this after school. What were you doing, anyway?"

"I was reading."

"Jason, I keep telling you, you've got to get out there and hustle."

"Yeah."

"Where have you applied so far?"

"Burger King, Taco Time, and Kentucky Fried Chicken."

"Well, what do they say?"

"They don't need anybody."

"Well you've got to go back there every few days or so and make yourself known to the manager. Make an impression — stand out!"

"Yeah."

"What'd you write on the applications? You've got to make that stand out, too."

"Just the usual stuff."

"Why'd you say you left your last job?"

"Robbery."

"What?"

"Robbery."

"You mean where it says, 'reasons for leaving last place of employment,' you just wrote down the word 'robbery'?"

"Yeah."

"Oh for crissake, Jason!"

Just then the microwave beeped (thank God). Saved by the bell! I took out my lasagna and dumped it out on a plate, got some milk, and sat down at the kitchen table and began eating.

It tasted pretty good, although I get tired of eating frozen stuff. That's about all we eat. One thing about frozen food is that the house never smells good like it does when you cook real stuff, like when there's real chicken in the oven or something, and when you get home you open the kitchen door and it smells great and you say "What're we having for dinner?" and the mother says "Chicken," and then you open the door of the oven and look at it and it's all golden brown and crispy and juicy and stuff.

Dad didn't say anything for a few minutes and I was happy thinking that today's job lecture was over. But it wasn't.

"Listen, Jason," Dad sat down next to me and opened a beer to drink with his stuff, "you've got to go back to all those places and fix up that application. You've got to go in those places and ask for the manager and then — here, stand up. I'll show you."

Dad stood up by the end of the table and stared down at me. "Come on, get up, Jason."

So I stood up and he whipped out his hand. "Hello," he said with this phony smile on his face, "I'm Jason Kovak — be sure and look the guy right in the eye, Jason, and have a firm handshake, a handshake tells everything about a person, right off. You have to have a firm grip, like this," he said, practically squeezing my hand to death. "And look the guy right in the eye — right square in the eye. Got it?"

"Yeah." I sat down as soon as I could pry my hand out of his.

"Then, Jason, you ask for the application and say there's been a change since you first filled it out. Then you fix up the part about why you left your last place of employment."

"Fix it? Like how? I left Wendy's because of the robbery. That's why I left."

"Dammit, Jason, don't you see how that looks to an employer? I mean if they don't think you robbed the place yourself they might think you left because you were suspected of a robbery or that you left because they had a robbery and you are a chickenshit and you can't take the heat."

"That's exactly what I am!" I took the lasagna and dumped it in the sink. Then I headed for the door.

72

"Where are you going?"

"I'm getting out of here!"

"Jason!"

I slammed the door. The hell with him. He leaves whenever *he* feels like it. I got in my car and backed out of the driveway. It screeched as I put it into gear.

I didn't know where I was going — I just started driving around. When I got to the corner of 34th and McClellan I turned left, away from Rainier Avenue and all the fast-food places. I drove past Mt. Baker Park. I turned left again at Lake Park Drive and went down to Lake Washington Boulevard, which runs along right next to the lake. There was a fair amount of traffic, people getting home from work and stuff, and a lot of people who run after work were on the jogging trail. I just kept on driving until Lake Washington Boulevard ended at Seward Park. I turned left at the park and drove all through it. It's a beautiful park. All the parks in Seattle are beautiful. This one has huge, tall evergreen trees that cover the entire point of land that sticks out into the lake. The park road makes a big loop and when I came out I was back where I had started. I just kept driving around until I ended up at the playfield on Genesee Street. Dad used to watch me play soccer there. I looked across the playfield. There were some little-kid soccer teams practicing. It looked like fun. At the end of the field I saw the post office and I thought about the ads I had answered.

I drove over there and decided to go in and check

my box. What the hell — it had been almost a week since I sent those letters. It was something to do.

I parked the car in the lot, got out my key to check the number again, and then found my box.

I couldn't believe it! Inside there were two envelopes: one addressed to Jason Kovak and the other to T. Worthington Jones.

CHAPTER 7

I GRABBED the letters and charged out of the post office, leaping down the stairs, three at a time.

"Watch yourself, sonny!" This big fat guy yelled at me as I flew by him.

"Uh, sorry, sir." (Watch it yourself, you big gorilla.) I jumped in the car and flipped on the radio. They were doing a salute to the Beatles and they were playing "Here Comes the Sun." Definitely a good sign for my future, even though it was raining.

For a few minutes I just stared at both envelopes. Then I tore open the one addressed to Jason Kovak. The letter shook in my hands as I read it.

> Dear Mr. Kovak,
>
> I received your reply regarding the consultant position for which I placed an advertisement in the Weekly newspaper. I would like to have you come to my home, 1212 Shoreland Dr. S, for an inter-

*view on Thursday, September 30, at 4:00. If you
are unable to meet with me at this time, please let
me know so that we may arrange for another time
that is mutually convenient. If I don't hear from
you, I will expect you Thursday, September 30, at
four o'clock. I look forward to meeting you.*

Sincerely,
Bertha Jane Fillmore

I read the letter one more time. And then about
five more times. I have an interview! I have a real job
interview! I pounded the steering wheel and turned
the radio up louder. I couldn't wait to tell Dad. Then
I stared at the other letter. It really was addressed to
T. Worthington Jones — his name was typed right
on the envelope. *What am I getting myself into?* I better
read this in the privacy of my own home, I thought,
as I put the car in reverse. The tires screeched a bit as
I tore away from the curb.

Driving home, all of a sudden, I was feeling weird.
I thought about Dad. Would he still be there? I had
been so mad when I left. As I drove along the lake, I
kept watching all the cars that passed me. I kept
looking for a red Corvette.

When I got home, his car was gone and the house
looked empty. To tell you the truth, I hate Dad
hassling me all the time about a job, but I felt bad
when I didn't see his car. I started thinking about
how it used to be.

We used to do stuff together, just the two of us.
When I was younger he'd help me make models —

stuff like that. And ever since I can remember we'd watch the Seahawks on TV on Sundays and sometimes he'd get tickets for us to go to the Kingdome to watch 'em play. Just us — Mom never liked it much. But since she left, he's never around. It pisses me off. I know it must have been crummy for him to have her run off with That Fruitcake, but with Mom gone, I would have thought he'd have wanted the two of us to stick together a lot more.

I went down to my room and flopped down on my bed. I held the letter to T. Worthington Jones up to the light. You know, some people are the type that tear open packages and presents right away. And other people shake them, rattle them, stare at them, and then finally open them — they torture themselves. I'm like that. I actually smelled the letter. I wondered if the lady put perfume on it. Then I imagined her typing the name on the envelope with her nice little hands and licking the envelope and pressing down firmly on it to seal it and then licking the stamp with her nice little tongue. Finally, when I couldn't stand it anymore, I tore it open.

The first thing I looked at was the signature. I had memorized the ad she had put in the *Weekly*. I knew the entire thing, each word. (Take my hand, let's feel the magic, dark-eyed beauty, classy and sharp, seeks devilish gentle male. Age not important.) But I had also imagined a person named Pamela being the dark-eyed beauty. I was really shocked when I read the signature and saw that it was from a "Lisa."

Then it hit me! A real live person had written this letter! We're talking an alive lady here. I mean, this letter was not from my imagination, it was from a real person! (Oh my God.) The minute this dawned on me goosebumps exploded up all over my body.

Dear Mr. Jones:

Isn't this just a fun way to meet people! I really enjoyed getting your letter. Your travels sound wonderful! I'd just love to get together while you're in town. I want to hear all about your climbing Mt. Everest. I just think that's so exciting. I'm a legal secretary with Weinberg, Carlotti, and Wong. They're a law firm whose offices are downtown in the Seattle First National Bank building. There's a lovely restaurant and bar on the top floor of the building, The Mirabeau. The view is spectacular. I could meet you there at 4:30 on Friday, October 8. I have dark hair and dark eyes and I'll be sitting in the bar, wearing a red dress. If this doesn't work out for you, just drop me a line and let's see what else we can cook up.

Looking forward to meeting you!

Lisa LaRue

Lisa LaRue — what a name!

"See what else we can cook up." Yes, yes, yes, Lisa, my darling!

I lay there on my bed imagining her. I could see her right there in front of my eyes. She looked just like Pamela — the same magnificent body, a beautiful face with a warm mouth that had a tongue in it,

and some nice teeth. Smoldering dark eyes, long silky
dark hair, long slim fingers — which would grab me.
(Oh my God.)

What the hell should I do? This is a real person, a
legal secretary! A legal secretary named Lisa LaRue!

I leaped out of bed with the letter and I rummaged
around through the Tintin books on my desk. I found
Tintin in Tibet and stuck the letter in the back of it.
Then I put it on the bottom and piled all the other
Tintin books all over it. I felt a little better after that.
I went back to my bed, where I had left the letter to
Jason Kovak. I was a little less panicky now that I
had Lisa LaRue temporarily under control, buried
under all my Tintin books, so I sat on my bed and
read the letter from Bertha Jane Fillmore one more
time.

After I finished reading it, I put it down and I said
to myself, "Jason, T. Worthington Jones will just
have to wait."

"That's for sure. I don't know what in the hell to
do about Lisa LaRue!

"But Jason Kovak needs a job. Burger King is not
exactly breaking down your door. You better get to
Bertha Jane Fillmore's house on Thursday."

Just then I heard the garage door opening. Dad
was back. For some screwy reason, I wanted to run up
the stairs and jump on him like I used to do when he
came home from work when I was about five years
old. Stupid, I know, but that's what I thought about
just then. Dad would come home and I'd run and do

a flying tackle and then he'd pick me up and tickle me. I'd laugh like hell and he'd carry me into the living room and we'd wrestle around on the floor and stuff — just the two of us, while Mom made dinner. Sometimes I'd ride around on his back like he was a horse. It was great.

But I didn't go upstairs. I went over to my stereo and I put on a record. Then I put on my earphones and I just lay on my bed with my earphones on, listening to the music with my eyes closed.

I wanted him to come downstairs. But he didn't. I lay there like that for the whole side of the album. When the last song was over, I took off my earphones and turned off my stereo. I was starving again, so I went up to the kitchen to get something to eat.

Dad was sitting at the kitchen table. He was drinking a beer and reading the paper. He looked up when I came in the kitchen.

"Jason?"

"Yeah."

"Uh, listen I'm, uh, I'm sorry I've been pushin' you so hard about the job."

"Uh-huh."

"It's just that I want you to make something out of yourself."

"Uh-huh."

"I'll try and back off a little."

"Well, I got an interview."

"Really?"

"Yeah, it's for a good job. The interview's on Thursday. I saw the ad for it in the paper and I sent in an application. I got a letter today about an interview."

"Way to go, son!" Dad jumped up and started thumping me on the back. "That's great! I knew you could do it. Just go for it, Jason!" He whacked me on the back some more and then he finished his beer and took his keys out of his pocket. "Well, I gotta be on my way — got a date. You'll be okay, right, Jason?"

"Yeah."

"Listen, I'm just going out for a drink. I should be back around nine. When I get home, we'll need to get you prepared for that interview."

"Huh?"

"Sure, we'll do some mock interviews just like they do at the Northwest Institute. See you later, Jason."

I made myself a sandwich and then I went down to my room and read the letters again. The one about the job interview was starting to worry me. Bertha Jane Fillmore, whoever that was, hadn't said anything in the letter about the job. I wondered how Dad would make me rehearse for a job interview when we didn't even know what kind of job it was.

At nine o'clock, I heard his car in the garage and in a few minutes he yelled down the stairs.

"Jason!"

"Yeah."

"Are you ready? Come on up so we can get going."

"Okay." I wondered how I could get out of this.

Upstairs, Dad said we should go into the den where there was a desk. I followed him in there and he shut the door behind me. I was trapped.

"Now, Jason, the first thing you do is get there early. First impressions are everything. Got that? Everything!"

"Uh-huh." My first impression of this situation was to leave.

"Now, you've gotten there early, right? And the first thing you do when the guy calls you to his office —"

"It's a lady."

"A lady?"

"The letter I got about the interview is signed by Bertha Jane Fillmore. I think it's a lady."

"Oh. Okay. Now the first thing you do when the lady — say, what kind of a job is this anyway?"

"I don't know." I'd been afraid he'd ask that.

"What did it say in the letter?"

"It just said when to come for the interview and the only thing it said about the job was that it's for a consultant."

"A consultant? Hmmm . . ."

"Maybe we shouldn't bother doing this."

"Well it is hard to imagine a sixteen-year-old boy being a consultant. But they've seen your application and want to interview you, so they must have seen something they like."

"We don't really know much about the job. Maybe we should just skip the rehearsal, Dad."

"Oh no, interviewing skills are important to have. You need to know how to handle yourself, Jason. Now the first thing you do when the guy — I mean, the lady — calls you into her office is walk in, look her right in the eye, and give her that firm hand-shake. Remember?"

"Uh-huh." Hand-crunching time again.

"Now try it. Go out of the den and I'll call you in."

I went out of the room and Dad shut the door. Then he opened it.

"Jason Kovak?"

I walked into the den. This whole thing was so stupid I couldn't believe it.

"Firm handshake, now, Jason, remember."

I stuck out my hand and Dad crunched it. "I'm Jason Kovak."

"I'm glad to meet you, I'm Bertha Jane Fillmore," said my dad. "Have a seat." Dad went behind the desk and I sat in the chair across from him.

"Now, Jason, we were most interested in your application," Dad said, holding the telephone book in front of him. "Can you tell me what your strengths are? What special qualities you'll bring to our organization?"

"Uh, I don't know."

"All right, now this is important, Jason. You've got to sell yourself."

"Dad, I really don't want to do this anymore. I don't have any special qualities — and —"

Dad looked at his watch. "Okay, let's knock off for tonight. But, of course, you have some good qualities. And tomorrow when we practice, I want you to be ready to tell me about them."

The whole week went like that. Dad would go in the den and shut the door while I waited in the living room, then he'd call me in and we'd shake hands and I was supposed to tell him how great I was. That's where I always got stuck. I could never think of anything. On Wednesday night in interview rehearsal, the night before I was supposed to meet with the real Bertha Jane Fillmore, Dad started sounding irritated.

"Jason, of course you have strengths!"

"Like what?"

"Well, all right. You always got to work at Wendy's on time didn't you?"

"Yeah."

"Okay. See? You're punctual. And you were nice to people, weren't you?"

"I guess so."

"See — punctual, courteous — get the idea? Now let's try it again. Jason, what strengths do you have to bring to our organization?"

"Uh, I'm punctual and courteous."

Dad didn't say anything for a few minutes. "I guess that's about as far as we're going to get." He didn't sound too pleased. "Just remember, tomorrow's the big day. Try hard. Sell her on you, Jason. Go for it!"

On Thursday the whole day dragged. Every class at school seemed like it was about five hours long, even P.E. After the last bell, I was at my locker when Kenny walked by.

"How's it going, Jason?"

"I don't know, man. I have a job interview this afternoon and, as you know, talking to people isn't one of my great strengths."

"Yeah."

"I think talking to you and talking to myself is about my limit. I'm pretty nervous."

"Well, good luck, Jason."

"Thanks."

After Kenny left, I got in my car and drove to the address given in the letter. It was on a street that had some big old mansions on it. Actually, it wasn't that far from my house. I got there really early like Dad said and I brought the newspaper so I could read the sports page while I waited.

I parked across the street from the driveway. On either side of it there were two stone posts — one of them had the house number etched on it. I couldn't see the house from the street, because the driveway curved around and there was this huge laurel hedge, I mean huge — it looked over nine feet tall, like a green wall on either side of the driveway. It blocked everything.

I picked up the paper, but before I turned to the sports page this headline caught my eye. TEEN KILLED IN MODELING SCAM. The article said a sixteen-year-old girl from Bellevue had answered a help-wanted ad for a fashion model and had been killed by this maniac when she met the guy at his so-called office.

I put the paper down. I was really spooked. Whoever Bertha Jane Fillmore was, she hadn't said anything in the letter about what this job — *if it really was a job at all* — was all about. What if Bertha Jane Fillmore was really a man? A sex pervert who put ads in the paper to trick people?

Maybe it would be a good idea for me to just turn around and go home. That seemed, in fact, like quite a sensible thing to do. But then I thought about Dad.

"Jason, just do it. It's almost four o'clock. Just go right up there and ring the bell. If there's a weirdo in there, just punch the scumbag in the stomach and run."

That really didn't convince me but when I thought about having to tell Dad that I had chickened out, I got even more scared. I'd rather take my chances with the maniac. I got out of the car and crossed the street.

As I headed around the curve of the driveway, I saw the house itself. It was red brick with white columns in the front and black shutters on all the zillions of windows, and it had ivy growing all over the front of it. Attached to the house there was a three-car garage. I walked up the front steps. I took the letter out of my pocket. Then I rang the bell.

And then I waited.

And then I waited some more.

I rang the bell again, but still no one came. I was looking at the letter once more to make sure I had gotten the time and the date right, when the door finally opened.

I don't know exactly who I expected would answer the door. But I was real surprised to find myself looking down at a girl. I couldn't tell how old she was, but she looked like she could be around my age, and she was Asian. Well, I couldn't tell anything else about her, except for one thing — she was beautiful.

I just stood there. I didn't think she was Bertha

Jane Fillmore, but I didn't know who else she could be, or if I was even in the right place. I just stared at her.

"Hello." She opened the door wide.

"Uh — I'm, a- . . ." my voice sort of squeaked. I don't know what had happened to it. It hadn't done that for years. I held out the letter until I managed to croak out my name. "I'm Jason Kovak and uh — I —"

She nodded and motioned for me to come in.

Inside the house, I stood in a huge hallway. It had a gray-stone kind of tile floor and dark wood paneling on the walls. Everything about the place looked old and rich.

"Please wait," the girl said. Her voice was soft and she had an accent of some kind. She left the hallway quickly, and disappeared into the house.

It was quiet — like a tomb. Creepy. Then from somewhere inside the house I heard a clock bonging four o'clock, and at the same time a cuckoo clock going at it, and chimes going off — I mean all kinds of bonging and cuckooing, donging and dinging and squawking. I'd never heard anything like it. I figured the whole house must be filled with zillions of clocks all going nuts.

"Jason," I said to myself, "this is a weird place. The time has come to leave. I will just have to be known forever as Jason the Quick and the Not So Brave." I was tiptoeing toward the front door when a door to the hallway opened.

Standing in the doorway was a very little and very

old lady. She was leaning on a cane that was all carved and painted like a totem pole.

"You are prompt."

"Uh —"

"I like that," she said, in this nice little voice. "Come this way, Jason Kovak."

She turned and opened the door of the hallway. I thought for a minute about leaving but I was so much bigger than this old lady — she couldn't have weighed as much as my entire Joe Weider Weight Set. So I followed her into a huge, sunny living room. That's where I saw the clocks. They were all over the room; it almost looked like a clock store. The room had other stuff too. It had chairs and couches and tables and lots of fresh flowers in vases and a grand piano. A huge chandelier hung down in the center of the room and there were photographs in silver frames all over the place, every table filled with them. They were like family pictures, everywhere you looked, only they were pictures of animals.

And not just regular animals — like dogs or cats. They were portraits of apes and bears and fancy birds and lions and hippos. There were even pictures of some animals that were so strange, I didn't know what they were. The old lady saw me looking around at the pictures.

"I am a zoo parent."

"Oh." I had no idea what she was talking about.

"Come over here, Jason Kovak. We'll sit here under Millard's portrait." She motioned toward the fireplace where there were two chairs that looked like the kind of chair that guy on "Masterpiece Theatre" sits in. The chairs faced each other and over the fireplace there was a painted portrait. This one wasn't of an animal. It was of a fat, burly-looking old guy in old-fashioned clothes. He looked a little like Ray Malavasi, who used to be the coach of the Los Angeles Rams.

I sat down in the chair across from the lady, where I could really look at her for the first time. She actually looked like an old version of the Pillsbury Doughboy. She was little and white and soft and shriveled up. Except for her eyes. They were brownish green and they had flecks in them and they were real sparkly — they kind of stood out from her face, which was powdery white. Her hair was white too, and it stuck out in little white pieces all around her face — not punk looking, more like a halo or something. She had on a regular old-lady dress and brown shoes that tied. The dress was the same color that my mom decorated one of our bathrooms — lilac, I think she called it.

"Well, Jason Kovak, here we are. Sitting right under Millard." She glanced up at the portrait of the old guy. "It's quite fitting I think, don't you?"

"Uh, I guess so." I still had no idea what she was talking about.

"Oh, my stars, I didn't really introduce myself, did I?"

"Well — uh — not exactly."

"My memory. Tch tch," she clucked and shook her head. "Reminds me of the joke Harry used to tell. He used to say, 'My memory's the same, it's just my for-gettery that's gettin' better.' " She slapped her knee after she told this joke. Then she laughed a lot and I tried some polite laughing too.

"Now, where were we?"

"You mentioned about introducing yourself." I wondered when we were supposed to shake hands. Dad's rehearsals weren't doing me much good here.

"Oh, of course. You're a good boy, Jason, you stay right on the track. I like that. Right on the track."

"Uh-huh." I wondered if this was where I should start selling myself.

"Well, that's one of the things I need you for, my dear. To help me stay right on the track." Then she scowled and looked puzzled for a minute and brushed a piece of her hair from her forehead. "Oh land, I still haven't told you. I am Bertha Jane Fill-more."

"Hello." Maybe now I was supposed to say I'm punctual and courteous.

"Hello." She smiled at me and then looked up at the portrait over the fireplace. "We're related, Mil-lard and I." Then she just sat and beamed at me like I was supposed to know exactly who Millard was. It was the same way she had said she was a zoo parent, like everyone knew about this, knew all about exactly what she was talking about.

My face must have shown I didn't know, because as she looked at me her smile faded. All of a sudden she looked kind of sad.

"You don't know, do you?"

"Know?"

"Know who Millard Fillmore is?"

"No, Mrs. Fillmore, I'm sorry I —"

"Bertha Jane. Please call me Bertha Jane."

"I'd feel kind of silly. I mean —"

"I insist."

I just nodded. I didn't know what to say.

"Now, Jason. I will tell you. My relative, distant as we may be, but nonetheless, my relative, Millard Fillmore, was the thirteenth president of the United States of America."

"Oh, uh, I'm not so hot at history. I'm sorry."

"My dear boy, it's not just you. You mustn't feel badly. You see I am sorry to say that for those that know of Millard he's known as the most unknown president. There are others, as well, who think of him as the epitome of mediocrity. It does trouble me a bit, although it's not what you think. I don't really intend to win."

"Win?"

"Oh, not for president. For mayor."

I had a feeling I should head for the door. Everything was so screwy here. I think the old lady — I mean, Bertha Jane — saw me squirming around.

"Oh my stars, I haven't done very well explaining this 'tall." She scowled and then brushed some hair from her forehead. "I'll try and start at the beginning." Then she sighed and looked up at the portrait of the old guy for a minute. "Jason, I will turn eighty-one on November twenty-eighth of this year and as I look back, for the most part my life has been a good and productive one. But an elderly person must contemplate death, Jason, although I'm sure you're too young to fully appreciate that. However, in doing so I have felt that there are a number of things I must speak out on, a way I must be useful, try to be heard before my time is up. Do you understand?"

"Well, I don't know, exactly."

"No, I suppose not." She paused for a minute, then she said, "You see, I decided the mayor's race will be the perfect forum for me to present my ideas. And, of course, I certainly meet all the eligibility requirements. Residency — I've lived in Seattle my whole life; and, of course, the age requirement — I am old enough to be eligible." She chuckled when she said that.

I laughed politely.

Then the old lady — Bertha Jane — lifted up her cane and unscrewed the top of it. She pulled out a rolled-up piece of paper, put it on her lap, then screwed back the top of her cane.

"Quite a filing system, isn't it, Jason?" she said as she patted her cane.

"Uh-huh." Maybe now was the time to lay it on her about my punctual, courteous strengths.

She unrolled the piece of paper, spread it out on her lap, and smoothed it out with her hands. "This is your application, Jason. I had asked for a person's philosophy of life as I felt that would be an open-ended question that would give me the best sense of the people who applied. I must say yours was quite to the point — a bit on the brief side, but I felt right in tune with its message. After reading it, I made up my mind to hire you if you want the job."

I still didn't know what job she was talking about, but she went right on talking, so I didn't ask.

"Your reply to my ad is actually quite similar in style and tone and especially content with what I want to say in this election." Then Bertha Jane picked up the paper and held it in front of her. She cleared her throat and in a great booming voice (I almost fell into the fireplace) she read:

"PEOPLE SHOULD BE NICE TO EACH OTHER
THERE SHOULD BE NO BOMBS
A PERSON SHOULD TRY TO LAUGH SOME EVERY DAY
EVEN IF THERE ISN'T A BIG LAUGH EVERY DAY
A LITTLE ONE IS BETTER THAN NONE."

Then she put the paper down and in her normal soft voice she said, "I left out the last line you wrote. You said, 'That's about it.' I feel the message is stronger without that."

"Uh-huh." I decided to forget about selling myself.

"Jason, I'm going to be paying minimum wage for this job. The hours will be flexible, after school and sometimes on weekends, perhaps some evenings, too. And there will be some extra jack-of-all-trade-type duties, perhaps helping me in the garden and a few other things we can discuss later."

"Uh, in the paper the ad said it was for a consultant?"

"Yes. And now that I've met you in person, I can

tell you specifically that on last July first I went to the Municipal Building and I paid the filing fee and filed as a candidate for mayor of the City of Seattle," she glanced up at the portrait of the old guy over the fireplace, then she smiled at me, "and today, Jason Kovak, I'd like to offer you the position of manager of the Bertha Jane Fillmore for Mayor Campaign."

At that moment all the clocks went nuts again, bonging and dinging and donging and squawking. The one that seemed the loudest was the cuckoo.

CHAPTER 8

BERTHA Jane Fillmore wanted me to come back the next afternoon after school to begin my job. She said she'd go over it in more detail then. She asked me what time I could get there and I told her four o'clock. She said good. I said okay. Then I left, convinced I was as nuts as she was.

Driving home, I couldn't quite believe that I had said I'd go back, and that I was actually going to work for her. I mean, only two hours earlier I had been an unemployed lettuce chopper and now here I was, Jason Kovak, Campaign Manager for Loony Old Lady.

All the way home I kept telling myself that at least I was employed. The best thing about that was Dad — at least I could tell him I had a job. Besides that, whatever this thing with Bertha Jane Fillmore turned out to be, it couldn't be any worse than cutting up lettuce. I was sure of that (sort of).

Dad was watching the news when I got home. The minute he heard me unlock the door he came charging into the kitchen.

"How'd it go, Jason?"

"I got the job." I grinned. Even though it was a weird job, it was great telling him I got it.

"Terrific!" He whacked me on the back. "Did you do what I told you, like we practiced? Did you look the lady in the eye and give her a firm handshake right off?"

"Well — uh — not exactly."

"Oh. Well, I'm sure you must have made a strong impression in the interview. No doubt about that." Dad leaned back against the refrigerator and folded his arms across his chest. "You know, Jason, I think role-playing like we did is the real key. When you imagine the whole thing in your mind and walk through it step by step, and concentrate — that's the most important part, you know, the concentration, it's *the key* — then, by God, you can achieve anything. I learned that at the Northwest Institute and believe me, Jason, it works."

"Uh-huh."

"What kind of a job is this anyway?"

"I don't know."

"What? You still don't know?"

"I don't know exactly."

"You got the job but you don't know what it is?

Didn't you ask her? I mean, didn't she tell you, Jason?"

"Well, I don't know exactly what it is but I think it's helping the old lady with some stuff." (Like managing her campaign for mayor of Seattle.)

"Like a handyman?"

"Well she said it might kind of involve being like a jack-of-all-trades." (Allow for fudging the facts a bit, here.)

"Oh, well, that's okay, Jason. A guy's gotta start somewhere, gotta be willing to go anywhere do anything if you're gonna make it in this world." Then he slapped me on the back again. "Can't be picky, right, Jason!"

"Uh-huh." (Picky? Never!)

"Well, I'm going out for dinner tonight. You can fix yourself something, right?"

"Yeah." (Don't I always?) I opened the freezer and looked at all frozen stuff. I took out a waffle. "Dad?"

"Yes?"

"Do you know who Millard Fillmore is?"

"Sure. He's the most unknown president of the United States."

"Oh."

"See you later, Jason. Good going on getting that job!"

After Dad left I ate my waffle. Frozen waffles never taste as good as real ones. We used to have them on Sunday mornings when Mom lived here. Dad always made them. Sometimes we'd have pancakes, too. He liked to cook on Sunday mornings.

As I ate my waffle, I thought more about Bertha Jane Fillmore. At least that stuff was true about that guy Millard Fillmore — not that I thought she was any less loony, but at least she hadn't made that whole thing up.

I put more syrup on my waffle. I wondered, What does a campaign manager do, anyway? My God, I can't even talk to people — I mean, what if that old wacko wanted me to talk in front of people and make speeches and crap like that, standing up in front of people and saying, "Vote for Bertha Jane Fillmore! She's the best!"

I got so concerned thinking about this that I didn't realize I was drowning my waffle. The syrup was oozing and gushing everywhere and spilling over the sides of the plate onto the table. What a mess. It was disgusting.

While I was cleaning up all the sticky crap, the phone rang. I washed the goo off my hands and ran to get it. It was Kenny. I was hoping he might want to do something.

"Jason?"

"Hi, Kenny."

"Can you give me a ride to school tomorrow? My car died."

"Sure. I'll pick you up at seven thirty."

"Say, how was the job interview?"

"I got the job — but it's bizarre. Totally bizarre."

"Like how?"

"I'm working for this goofy old lady — she says she's running for mayor of Seattle and I'm supposed to be her campaign manager."

"You're kidding."

"I kid you not. She's definitely not firing on all cylinders."

"Nuts, huh?"

"Totally. But it's money. Only minimum, but I took it. At least it'll get Dad off my case for a while. She said besides managing her campaign, I'm also supposed to do yard work."

"Good luck, man."

"Yeah, well, I'll be there in the morning."

"Thanks."

I felt better after talking to Kenny, even if he had only called for a ride. I watched some TV and went to bed. I decided not to worry about being a campaign manager until I went to Bertha Jane Fillmore's house tomorrow for my first day of work. What the hell — there wasn't anything I could do about it right then anyway.

I must have been pretty successful at putting the whole thing out of my mind, because that night I had a dream that was so great that when the alarm went off I was mad that I had to stop dreaming and get up. It was about Lisa LaRue.

There we were, me and Lisa LaRue, romping along this deserted beach in our bathing suits. Hers was actually quite a small bathing suit and as we bounced and bounded along, the warm salt water lapped up over our legs and our knees and her thighs and stuff. Then I slide tackled her like in soccer and we frolicked in the waves and on top of the warm wet sand and I rolled over her and the surf pounded and pounded over us. And she said in between her panting, "Oh, Jason, you're such a devil!"

When I woke up, I ran over to my desk and looked under all my Tintin books to make sure Lisa LaRue was still under there. She was. I got excited seeing her letter right there, still stuck in the back of *Tintin in Tibet*. Then I glanced at the other books on my desk. *Getting Women to Want You: Handbook for the Single Male*, the latest addition to my collection, was on top of the pile. What *was* I really going to do about her? She expected to meet T. Worthington Jones, who just returned from Tibet, who climbed Mt. Everest, who has a yacht. There's no way she'd buy that once she met me.

In the shower I told myself that I had a week to come up with a plan. I sure hoped I could. In the meantime, I reminded myself, I was getting some great dreams out of the deal.

When I got to Bertha Jane Fillmore's house again at four that afternoon, the same girl let me in. She really was beautiful. I had noticed it the first time I saw her but she'd disappeared so quickly, and I had been so nervous, it hadn't hit me the way it did this time. She had long dark hair down to her shoulders and she was small. Her head came to the middle of my chest. I felt like an NBA power forward next to her. Her huge dark eyes reminded me of a deer's. She was quiet like that, too. She hardly said anything. I couldn't take my eyes off her at first — it was embarrassing. I expected her to dart away again, but this time she didn't disappear. She stood next to me in the hall. I felt my face getting red as I tried to stop staring at her. While we waited there for Bertha Jane Fillmore, neither of us said a word. Total silence: me trying to keep my eyes on the floor and her looking at the ceiling. Situations like that are enough to make me start sweating.

"Jason, dear boy. Right on time again," the old lady — I mean, Bertha Jane — said as she opened the hall door. "I just know I've made the right choice by hiring you!" Her face crinkled up as she smiled and she brushed a little piece of wispy white hair from her forehead. "Now, I want to introduce you to someone very special to me," she said, smiling at the girl. "Jason, I'd like you to meet Thao Nguyen."

We both mumbled hello and looked at the floor and the ceiling some more.

Then Bertha Jane Fillmore told me to follow her and the girl disappeared again.

"Let's chat out on the deck, Jason. Warm autumn days are a special gift and we just mustn't waste them inside. Don't you agree?"

"Uh-huh." If there's one thing I learned at Wendy's it was that the boss is always right. So I nodded and followed her through the living room to these doors that opened onto a big deck. There were some nice chairs and a little table out there and the

101

deck looked over a huge yard that seemed to go all the way down to the lake. There was a winding grassy path that seemed like it probably ended at the lake.

"In the autumn, when it has its blanket of golden leaves, it always seems to be a magic path to me," she said, pointing to it, "a lovely golden path. There's often gold in your back yard, you know."

"Uh-huh."

"Ahhh. Just smell the air, Jason. I call it Granny Smith air on a day like this. There's a clarity to it, and it's so tart and crisp, just like those wonderful apples."

"Uh-huh."

"Now, Jason. I just wasn't able to get to the iris bed in June this year the way I should have, so one of the things I want you to do is help me get at it. See over there?" She pointed toward the left of the yard.

"Uh-huh." I looked where she pointed. It did seem to be a mess. Maybe I would just be a gardener after all.

"Well, it's just a thick mass of weeds and the poor plants themselves are getting buried alive. I hate weeds. They can be so vicious and destructive!"

"Uh-huh."

"Of course, they are part of God's earth, but if I love the earth must I love weeds, too?" she asked.

"I don't know."

"No, I suppose those are difficult things to answer." She tapped her cane and unscrewed the top of it like she had the day before and took out a piece of rolled-up paper. She smoothed it out on her lap and

102

then pushed up her glasses, which had fallen down to the end of her nose. "Now, Jason, your duties will include helping me in the garden. Every day we'll have a different project. The list is practically endless, you know, but there will be some rewards. The late raspberries are ripening and we can make some raspberry tarts. That would be lovely, don't you think?"

"Yes." If food was part of this job, I was all for it.

"And then I want you to help Thao with her English. She hasn't been in this country long, Jason. She came last spring from Viet Nam and I am her sponsor. Thao lives here with me and I employ her to help me around the house. She also goes to school during the day. She's sixteen and she has no family here, Jason, except an uncle in California who is sponsored by a family there, I believe."

"I'm supposed to help her talk?" Me talk? I felt my face getting red again. So far all I'd been able to say to the boss was "uh-huh," and she wasn't young and beautiful like Thao.

"Yes. That will be one of your jobs. In fact, I'll get her right now and we can begin this afternoon." Bertha Jane popped up and disappeared into the house.

While she was gone I sat on the deck and wondered how long a drop it might be from the deck to the ground so I could escape into the bushes. Given that I can hardly talk to people myself — unless you count phrases like, I don't know, uh-huh, maybe, yes, okay, I guess so, and stuff like that — I couldn't see how I was going to help anybody else master the English

103

language. And the old lady hadn't said a thing about that business about running for mayor and my being a campaign manager. Maybe she had just made that up yesterday. She was so goofy, I really didn't know what to think. I was standing at the edge of the deck, staring down over the railing when they came back.

Bertha Jane was carrying a little pad of paper and a pencil. "Now, Jason," she said, "I want you to move the chairs around in a little circle so we can all hear each other."

"Okay." Jumping over the deck didn't seem to be much of an option, so I just moved the chairs like she had told me. Bertha Jane sat in the middle, between me and the girl.

"The first thing we must do is have you each learn each other's name," Bertha Jane announced. Then she turned to me. "Jason, there are many sounds in the Vietnamese language which are very hard for Americans to pronounce correctly, just as there are many sounds in the English language which are difficult for the Vietnamese to say." She took the little pad of paper and wrote in big letters:

THAO NGUYEN

"Jason, Thao's first name is pronounced like the sound 'ow' with a 'T' in front of it. It's like if you fell down and hurt yourself and you said 'ow!' That's the sound you want to make. Thao rhymes with 'how.'"

"Okay."

"Now I want you to try it."

I looked at the floor of the deck and then I said

"Thao" making it sound like "how." When I looked up, Thao was smiling at me. It knocked me out.

"Very good, Jason!" Bertha Jane's face crinkled up. "Now, we'll try your last name for him, Thao. It's much harder, isn't it?"

"Yes." Thao nodded.

"Nguyen, Jason, is very hard for us because of the 'N-G-U' letters together. It is pronounced 'we' as in 'here we go,' but then you put just a very slight 'N' sound in front of it so it sounds like 'N-we.' Now I want you to try that first part."

"Okay."

Then Bertha Jane said "ngu," which sounded like "nwee," and I said it after her a whole bunch of times.

"Now, Jason, put it together with the last part of Thao's name, 'yen,' which rhymes with 'ten.' So it sounds like 'N-weeyen.' "

"Nguyen," I said, making it sound just like Bertha Jane had said. Then to dazzle them both I smiled at Thao and I said, "Thao Nguyen." I kind of surprised myself, and Thao and Bertha Jane laughed.

After that Bertha Jane wrote in big letters:

JASON KOVAK

And we helped Thao with my name. The "s" sound was hard for her, and with the "ko" part of my name she tended to pronounce it more like the "ow" sound so it kind of sounded like cow vak. But finally she got the whole thing right. I never knew before how hard it was to say people's names. I was feeling

105

pretty good until Bertha Jane asked me to just talk to Thao, to ask her something. I sat there looking at the floor. I couldn't think of a damn thing.

"Uh —"

"Just ask anything, Jason, dear, anything at all."

I looked at the lake. Blank. I was totally blank. After what seemed like hours, I finally blurted out, "Where do you go to school?"

Thao looked at me like she didn't understand at all.

"Just ask again, Jason," Bertha said.

"Where do you go to school?" This time I said it real loud.

"Now, Jason," Bertha said softly, "you have just made a very common mistake. Thao is not deaf. Her hearing is perfectly normal, no hearing problem whatsoever. When she doesn't understand what you have said, you must repeat it more slowly, not more loudly."

"Oh, okay — uh — I'm sorry." My face got all red again. What a nerd.

"Jason, it's the most common mistake when we have a language barrier. People start shouting at each other as if somehow turning up the volume will solve the problem. You mustn't worry about it, but now you know."

This time, real slowly — with not talking loud at all — I asked Thao again, "Where do you go to school?"

"I go to Ingraham."

106

I couldn't believe it. That's my high school. It's kind of big and all, but I had sure never seen her there before. It was sort of a shock. I thought of her as being so strange and different and here she went to Ingraham.

"In ESL."

"Oh."

Bertha Jane put the pad of paper on the table. "Thao has just started school at Ingraham, Jason, in the English as a Second Language Program — ESL. Are you familiar with it?"

"Not really." I was embarrassed. I had heard of the ESL deal and I knew it was at our school but I just never paid any attention to anyone who was in it. The whole thing was so separate. You never saw those kids at football games or any of the school stuff. It was like they didn't exist.

"Well, Jason," Bertha Jane said, looking at her list again from her cane, "now I really must show you the car, and I think that should do it for today."

I didn't know what she was talking about, but I followed the old lady through all these rooms and then through a door that connected to the garage. I looked around for Thao but she had disappeared somewhere in the house. I sure hoped that part of my job wouldn't be fixing the old lady's car because I'm not exactly Mr. Goodwrench. I can change the oil and tires and basic stuff, but that's about it. I've never been one of those guys that messes around cars a lot.

107

She opened the door to a huge three-car garage. Inside was only one car. It was a beauty. I couldn't believe it — a 1939 Bentley.

"Jason, my brother, Harry, lived with me for many years. He died last February. I do miss him terribly." She brushed some hair off her forehead. "Oh my stars, it's a hard thing, isn't it? Missing a dear one like that. Well, this was Harry's car, and he did drive it. I did too, for many years, until my eyesight got so poor." Bertha Jane walked over and patted the side of the car. "Sometimes a person does need to know when to quit, don't you think, Jason? Well, anyway, one of your duties will be to drive me to the store and, of course, almost every Friday I have a doctor's appointment and I'll need you to take me there and wait for me. You do know how to drive, don't you, Jason?"

"Uh-huh." (Do I ever!)

"Well that's wonderful. And, Jason, I do have to be at the doctor's a terribly long time, sometimes up to two hours. If you'd like to use the car for your own purposes during that time and then come back for me, that would be fine."

"Okay." (I really couldn't believe this, I really couldn't. There I would be, me, Jason Kovak, the wimp, bombing around in an old Bentley every Friday afternoon!)

Bertha Jane Fillmore told me to come to work again at the same time Monday and so I said goodbye and left.

Driving home in my own car, I started imagining

what it would be like driving that Bentley. It was then I had the greatest idea of my life. The plan! I had the plan!

T. Worthington Jones would write Lisa LaRue and tell her that he would meet her next Friday. I'd show up in the Bentley, tell Lisa LaRue that I was Mr. T. Worthington Jones's driver and that T. Worthington Jones suddenly got real sick and couldn't make it, and I'd get to hang around and be with Lisa LaRue — good old "age not important" Lisa LaRue, with her great body. And she'd say, "Well, I'm sorry T. Worthington Jones couldn't make it, Jason — but you'll do just fine. Let's cook something up!"

(Yes, yes, Lisa — let's do!)

CHAPTER 9

"WELL, I just couldn't get to this in June when I should have. That's all there is to it." Bertha Jane sounded aggravated while she poked at the weeds with the end of her cane. I wondered what happened in June, but (of course, being me) I didn't ask.

"It's a miracle, isn't it?" She looked out over the trees.

"Huh?" I was clearing the leaves out of the flower bed and starting to dig up some of the weeds.

"Be sure and pull out all those long white roots of that stitch grass and clear a space around the iris roots."

"Okay." I was actually starting to like this job. I can do yard work pretty well and so far she hadn't given me anything else I couldn't handle. Even if she was dingy, she talked all the time and didn't seem to mind that I didn't.

"Jason, the miracle is that the beauty of the leaves that die in autumn will come back again when the leaves bloom in the spring. Don't you see? The beauty isn't lost forever, it never dies. Only each single leaf dies. I'm sure the goodness of the human spirit must be resurrected and live on in that way, too. Oh my stars, here's Josephine! Hello, old girl!" Bertha Jane reached down and stroked a calico cat that had scooted out of the bushes near the evergreen tree. "You haven't met her yet, have you, Jason?"

"No."

"She's terribly friendly and fond of most people. You do like animals, don't you?"

"Uh-huh."

"Good, because Thomas is around here somewhere, too. He's a good friend, quite decent to Josephine and, of course, I'm convinced they both have nine lives, even though he's a dog. Oh, there he is over by that old apple tree." Bertha Jane pointed to a tree by the path that led to the water. The one she called the magic golden path. There was a funny old black and white mutt there. He was sort of middle-sized and shaggy. He had his leg up and he was peeing on the tree.

"That old apple tree, which Thomas frequently thinks is a toilet, is an inspiration to me, Jason, it truly is. It's so old and gnarled, but its trunk and branches, they all represent the long ripening and growth of life itself. And that old tree still makes apples! Think of that!"

"Uh-huh."

"Now, Jason, when you're done with weeding the iris beds, I'd like you to come in and help Thao a bit. She has a school assignment and it's quite difficult for her."

"Okay." (Oh no.)

I knew this had been too good to be true. Maybe I could pull weeds in super slow motion so I wouldn't have time to be the English teacher. The whole idea was ridiculous, like asking a guy who is afraid of heights to teach someone skydiving. What a joke — except I didn't feel like laughing.

Bertha Jane went into the house and while I was very slowly prying out the weeds, I decided to think of something more pleasant — like how I was going to be the driver for T. Worthington Jones when I met Lisa LaRue. I thought I'd probably get a hat, like a chauffeur's hat, and I could wear black slacks and a white shirt, kind of like a uniform. Maybe the hat would make me look older — and especially gentle and devilish, since that's what Lisa LaRue wanted. And Lisa gets what Lisa wants. (Yeah!) I could sort of have it pushed back on my head, or maybe cocked over one eye a bit. God, she'd love it.

"Jason!" Bertha Jane called down from the deck.

"Huh?"

"That's enough for today on the weeds, dear. Thao will meet you in the den."

"Okay." I guessed there wasn't any way I was going to get out of it. I gathered up the tools and took them to a shed that was attached to the garage.

While I put them away I peeked through the garage window at the Bentley. What a car — I still couldn't believe it! I bet women would run after me for miles when I was driving that car. I could smile and give them nice little waves as I drove by. I could just see this whole pack of women chasing after me as I rolled along in the Bentley. These women would all be bouncing along by the back bumper, led, of course, by none other than that classy dark-eyed beauty herself — Lisa LaRue.

I washed my hands in a big concrete sink in the toolshed and then went into the house. I wasn't sure where the den was. Bertha Jane Fillmore's house was so awesome, I still didn't know my way around it. The door from the garage led to a hallway next to the kitchen. I smelled something good, so I went in there.

Bertha Jane was bent over the stove. The oven door was open and she was taking out a cookie sheet filled with cookies.

"Do you like chocolate chip, Jason?"

"Yes." (My favorite, to be exact.)

While Bertha Jane was taking the cookies out of the oven, I noticed the bowl and spoon she'd used to make the cookie dough. Mom always let us lick those. It had been years since she made cookies, but you don't forget things like that. Sometimes I'd get to lick the bowl, and my brother, Jeff, got the spoon, or the other way around. No matter whether I got the spoon or the bowl, I always thought Jeff got more of the good stuff.

Bertha Jane saw me eyeing the bowl. "Jason, would you like to lick the bowl and the spoon?"

"Yes." (I certainly would.)

"Well, have at it, dear," she said, handing them to me.

"Thanks." This was the first time in my life I got to lick both. I felt slightly greedy. "Uh, do you think Thao would like to lick some, too? I could just take the spoon — she could have the bowl."

"No, dear. She's not overly fond of raw cookie dough, but she does like the finished product."

"Oh." I ran my finger around the bowl and popped the dough in my mouth.

"Jason, dear, this assignment Thao has, it's quite a struggle for her. It's painful. Be gentle."

"Okay." (Wimps are always gentle.) I wondered what this assignment was — but mostly I just wished Bertha Jane would change her mind about the whole thing. If she only knew what a joke it was to have me help someone talk.

"She has to write quite a detailed essay in English about how she came to America. You know, Jason, I have lived through two world wars, the Great Depression, the Korean War, and the Viet Nam War, but my life has been comfortable, like so many Americans'. I think it is difficult for us to fully appreciate a life experience that is so different from our own. Empathy is limited. We can never really know what life is like for another person, but we must keep on trying, nevertheless." Bertha Jane handed me the plate of cookies. "These are nice and warm. You can take these in the den for you and Thao."

"Okay — uh — just where's the den?"

"Oh my stars, Jason, it's just my forgettery getting better again!" She cracked up again when she said this. "I'd forgotten I hadn't given you a proper tour of the house. Maybe tomorrow we'll do it. But right now I'll just show you the den."

"Okay."

"Of course, beauty and goodness and the very earth itself won't last if we destroy it, Jason."

"Huh?" (Now what was she talking about?) It was so weird about her. Sometimes she made sense, but then she'd say something that would just seem off the wall.

"What we were speaking about in the yard."

"Oh yeah."

"I must make a very good speech about it, Jason."

"Uh-huh." (Did she mean that wacky mayor business?)

"Well," she brushed a piece of hair from her forehead and took off her apron, "run along to help Thao."

"Okay — uh, Mrs. Fill — I mean, Bertha Jane?"

"Yes, Jason?"

"Could you show me where the den is?"

"Oh my forgettery!" She cracked up all over again. She seemed to like this joke a lot. I have noticed that old people say the same stuff over and over again.

I followed her down a long hall and then into a

room that was like a huge library. There were bookshelves on every wall and at the end of the room there was a door.

She took a cookie off the plate and took a little bite as she pointed to the door. "The den is right in there."

"Thanks." As I walked across the room, I ate one of the cookies and wondered if Bertha Jane Fillmore was actually serious about running for mayor. She hadn't said a thing about it Friday and she was so goofy sometimes, it was hard to tell. Then I ate another one of the cookies. They were good. They were as good as Mom's.

Thao was sitting at a writing table, staring at a notebook. Her shoulders slumped down and she seemed sad. I didn't feel so hot myself. I couldn't imagine me teaching anybody anything. A chair was pulled up next to her. I figured I was supposed to sit there. The den was a nice room. It had a fireplace, a big overstuffed couch, and shelves lined with books. Josephine was curled up on Thao's lap.

"Hi, Thao." (Here goes nothing.)

Thao looked up at me. Her eyes were so pretty I had to look away.

"Hi, Jason," she said quietly.

I put the plate of cookies down on the table. "Want one? Bertha Jane made them for us." I tried to talk real slowly.

"Yes. Good." She smiled.

I sat down next to her and we ate the cookies and didn't say much.

116

Thao kept petting Josephine. "Cat very nice," she said softly.

"Yes, it is a nice cat," I said. I wasn't sure what I was supposed to do, so I just kept stuffing cookies in my mouth.

There was a long silence. Finally, Thao said, "I must do this." She pointed to a ditto sheet in the notebook that read:

ESL Class Assignment.
Part I   Essay Topic: How I Came to America
Part II   Read Essays to Class
Assignment Due Friday

Thao looked down at Josephine and kept petting her. "In Viet Nam I study English in school. I can read some and write some, but not talk good. When I try to write how I came to America I remember bad things, then I forget English words."

"Oh." I didn't know what to say.

"I afraid I fail." Thao sounded upset.

"The teacher's afraid he'll fail, too," I mumbled.

"What you said, Jason?"

"Oh, nothing." I didn't want to repeat it. I didn't know what to do. I started talking to myself:

"Think of something to say, Kovak."

"Yeah, like what?"

"I dunno — anything — there's gotta be somewhere to start."

"Like where?"

"Just think of something — anything!"

Thao and I just sat there not talking, with me arguing with myself. It was awful. Finally, Bertha Jane stuck her head in the door. "How's it coming, you two?"

I got red and Thao just looked down at the cat.

"Having trouble getting started, I see. Well, I've got an idea. Thao, why don't you tell Jason in your own words how you came to America and he can ask you questions. Like an interview, Jason."

"And then I could write down what Thao says and make the English words right." I smiled.

"Wonderful, Jason. Then Thao can practice reading it and you can help her with pronunciation."

"I can be like a reporter." I liked that idea.

"Well, I'll let you get to work. Do you have enough cookies?"

We both said yes at the same time and then looked at each other and laughed — kind of nervously.

"Are you ready to start, Thao?" I asked slowly, as Bertha Jane left.

"Okay." She still seemed kind of upset, but I was feeling better. Asking questions seemed easier than trying to think of things to say. I took some paper from her notebook and she handed me a pencil.

I wasn't sure where to begin. Finally, I asked, "Where did you live in Viet Nam?" That seemed like as good a place as any.

"Saigon."

I wrote down "Saigon" and looked over at Thao, waiting for her to go on, but she didn't say anything else. I waited . . . nothing but silence.

"I afraid I fail, Jason."

"No you won't. I just need to ask the right questions, okay?"

"Okay."

"Who did you live with?"

"My parents."

I wrote down, "I lived with my parents in Saigon," and then showed it to Thao.

"That look good." Thao smiled a little bit as she read the sentence.

"See, you won't fail."

She nodded and took a deep breath. Then softly she said, "I was live with my parents in Saigon. My father own small factory. The Communists take my father's company, our house, everything."

"They took everything you owned?"

"Yes. All we have left is clothes, things like that. A few gold rings we hid."

I had to ask Thao to repeat a few words and wait while I wrote down what she said. She talked slowly, so that helped. Then she got stuck again, so I showed her what I had written. When she finished reading it, she put it down and looked up at me. "You ask question, Jason. I don't know what to tell next."

"Okay. How did you escape?"

"Boat."

"No, I mean before that."

"Before that?" She looked confused.

"I mean, how did you get to the boat?"

"Oh. It like this, Jason. To escape Viet Nam you must pay secret person. My mother sold things we

119

had left at market — clothes, shoes, makeup — things like that. She buy and sell, buy and sell, for two year to get money to give to secret person."

"Enough for all of you to come to America?"

She didn't answer. I looked over at her, but she was looking away.

"Only me," she said after a long while. "As soon as they get enough money they want me to get out right away. My father, my mother, they tell me I must leave. They tell me they come later. I not want to leave them there, but they make me leave."

Thao waited while I wrote down, "My parents made me leave them in Viet Nam."

She was quiet for a long time. Finally, she said, "The money my mother get for me after two year is four piece of gold. My parents give gold to secret person. Secret person tell my parents I must travel to Long Khanh. I must go at night, wear dark clothes. It take seven hour. I say good-bye to my parents. I so scared. I don't know when I see them again."

Thao got up and walked over to the window and stood there while I wrote. When she came back, I saw tears in her eyes.

"Do you want to stop, Thao?"

"No. Must go on."

"Maybe this is enough for a start."

"No!"

"I'm sorry Thao — I just —"

"I must do well in school. I must do well for my parents!" Thao's face was flushed. "Ask question, Jason, ask question, now."

I tried to think of a question to ask her. I couldn't think of anything at first, but finally I said, "What did you take with you?"

"I take small bag with two pant, two blouse, underwear, and dry food." She spoke quickly.

"Dry food?"

"It like Communist food, like chocolate bar but not chocolate. They say it make you full all day, *luong kho*, it Chinese food. I have two of those, enough for two day and also little box with lemon and sugar mixed up. When you have no water you chew that. I wear gold rings. I go to house then I go to another house. We go in *xe lam*."

"What is that?"

"Uh, I can't think of word." Thao looked around the room, then she said, "Oh, yes, small bus, that right word. *Xe lam* is small bus. In small bus no one talks. No one know other people. We wait at last house six hours. At three a.m. someone comes. We follow to place near the river where the boat is to come. The river go to ocean. We hide with really high grass around us. We wait for boat to come. No one talks. Then I hear a loud voice. *NGOI IM KHONG DONG DAY!*"

"What does that mean?"

Thao looked blank. She must have been having trouble again remembering the English words. I wasn't sure what to do. I put my pencil down and waited.

Then she said, so softly I could hardly hear her, "It mean 'nobody move,' it is police. There are ten of

121

them. They have long guns. They make us get up. Police all around us." Then she talked real fast. "They make us walk. We go to jail."

"Jail?" I wasn't sure I heard the word right. *Had Thao really been in jail?* I stopped writing. "Jail — like a prison?"

"Yes, that place. They make me stay there three month. Older people stay longer. Sometime two, three year." Her voice broke.

Then she got up and walked quickly out of the room. I wrote down, "When I tried to escape, I was captured and spent three months in jail."

I sat alone in the den, staring at the paper. I didn't know what to do so I just waited there.

About ten minutes later Thao came back and stood in the doorway. Her eyes were red.

"Thao, really, maybe this is enough for today. We can work on the essay tomorrow when I come."

"Yes, okay, Jason. You make words right."

"I will, Thao."

"I go upstairs now."

I took the empty cookie plate out to the kitchen and rinsed it off. I had a knot in my stomach. The kitchen clock said six o'clock — time for me to leave. Bertha Jane had said she wouldn't need me any later than six today. But I wanted to go back to Thao, I wanted to say something, but I didn't know what. As I was leaving, Bertha Jane came out to my car. Thomas and Josephine were trotting along next to her.

"You were most helpful to Thao, dear. She needed

someone to help her break the ice. When she tried it on her own she seemed to forget every English word she knew. It was most upsetting to her."

"What I wrote down on that paper was real," I said quietly.

"Yes, Jason."

"Those things really happened to her."

"She misses her parents terribly, Jason. Especially her mother."

"Will she ever see them again?"

"She hangs on to that hope. But no one knows."

When I got home I went down to my room and put on my stereo. I couldn't stop thinking about Thao. I lay on my bed with my earphones on for a while. Then I decided to call Mom. I hadn't talked to her since I had been over there using her typewriter. I dialed her number. It just kept ringing and ringing. I figured she wasn't home and was about to hang up when she answered it.

"Hello?" She sounded kind of out of breath.

"Hi, Mom."

"Jason. Well, hello there."

"The phone rang a long time — I was about to hang up —"

"I was getting some chairs from the deck, honey. How are you?"

"Okay, I guess."

"Well, what have you been up to, Jason?"

"Not much, well, except I got a new job."

"You're not working at Wendy's anymore?"

"Nope."

"Oh. Are you working at another fast-food place?"

"Nope. I work for an old lady."

"That's nice, Jason. You'll have to tell me about it sometime."

"Mom?"

"Yes?"

"Uh, could I come over?"

"Oh, Jason, I'm so sorry, dear, but Roger and I are having some clients of his over for dinner tonight and I'm right in the middle of getting everything ready right now. In fact, I can't stay on the phone, honey. But I'm glad you called first. Maybe some other time, Jason."

"Okay."

"Good-bye, dear."

I hung up the phone. Then I heaved the damn thing against the wall. I grabbed this heavy-metal album and put it on and turned my stereo up full blast. Mom used to get so pissed when I'd do that.

I listened to it until it even started getting on my nerves. I went upstairs to get something to eat.

When I walked in the kitchen, the side door opened. Dad was home from work.

"Hi, Jason." Dad walked over to the refrigerator and took out a beer.

"Hi."

"Think I'll watch the news." He went in the living room and turned on the TV. I made myself a sandwich and then I went in and sat down next to him. We didn't talk until the commercial came on.

"Dad?"

124

"Yeah, Jason?"

"I called Mom today and she —"

"Jason, you know what? I think we ought to think of something cheerful to talk about. Know what I mean?"

"I guess so." (Hell — isn't there anyone I can talk to?)

"Now, how do you think the Huskies will do this weekend against UCLA? Aren't they having a great year?"

"Yeah, I guess so," I mumbled and walked out. Dad didn't even seem to notice.

I got in my car. I didn't know where I was going. I just drove around the neighborhood. I drove along Lake Washington Boulevard and through Seward Park. Then for some reason, I drove to Bertha Jane's house. I parked the car across the street. I couldn't see the house because of the hedge, but I imagined Bertha Jane and Thao having a nice dinner in the kitchen, where it smelled good. They were probably talking about things, Bertha Jane saying things like she does about the flowers and the earth, and Thao patting Josephine and saying things in her soft voice. I wanted to go in, but I wasn't supposed to go there until tomorrow. "You just work there, Kovak," I told myself. So I sat outside. Finally I drove home.

I went down to my room. I was feeling bummed out so I listened to some tunes, but I got sick of that and sick of feeling lousy.

"Lighten up, man," I said to myself.

"Yeah, how?"

"Lisa LaRue."

"What about her?"

"Think of good old Lisa LaRue. The one subject that gives you a real lift (ha!). It always works."

So I did. And it did this time, too. I made myself concentrate on her very hard, focusing on every little detail of her delicious self. The hell with everything, I thought — soon I would be submerged in lust as I lay in the hot grasp of the lovely Lisa LaRue. I most definitely started to feel better just thinking about this. Maybe Dad was right, maybe there was something to this concentration thing. In my mind Lisa LaRue and I were now lying clutched in each other's arms, consumed and overwhelmed with this lust, panting a lot.

And now, I thought, the time has come. Time to concentrate on some real action. "Jason," I said to myself, "now that you have figured out this driver thing, you must answer her letter."

I decided — no arguments — to write her a letter right then and there. This letter from T. Worthington Jones would tell her that he (Jason, the Quick and the Brave) would meet her at the Mirabeau Friday afternoon, just like she had suggested. I took off my earphones and went over to my desk and got Lisa LaRue out from under the Tintin books. I reread her letter to me and then I wrote to her.

Dear Lisa,
I hope you don't mind if I address you by your first name. What a lovely name and I was most

impressed to learn that you are a legal secretary
with the firm of Weinberg, Carlotti, and Wong.
That must be most interesting work. I was de-
lighted that you wanted to get together during my
layover in Seattle while my yacht is being repaired
and the Mirabeau sounds like a good choice of a
place for our first meeting. I hope it will be the first
of many such meetings. I will meet you there Friday
in the bar at 4:30 as you suggested. I anticipate
with pleasure making your acquaintance.

Sincerely,
T.W.

I had always thought a rich guy like T. Worthington Jones was probably called T.W. by his friends, so
that's how I signed it. Also I decided to go to an
army-navy store to get a navy or air force hat and
take the insignia off to make it look like a driver's hat.
Then I'd be all ready for Friday.

That night I had another dream about me and
Lisa LaRue. It was a lot like the last one I had about
her only it omitted the bathing suits. Man, were we
cooking it up!

CHAPTER 10

THE next day at school Kenny had lunch with me because Stephanie was sick. We were coming out of the lunchroom when Thao passed us in the hall.

"Hi, Jason." She smiled up at me.

"Hi, Thao. See you this afternoon."

"At four?"

"Right — see you then."

Kenny's jaw dropped open. "Who was that, man?"

"Thao Nguyen — she's from Viet Nam."

"How do you know her?"

"She lives with the old lady I work for. Part of my job is to tutor her in English." I smiled.

Kenny whistled. "I can't believe you, Kovak — you call that work? Getting paid to hang around a girl who looks like that — some job!"

"Not bad, huh?" I was grinning now.

"I'll say. How's that old lady, anyway? You said she was nuts."

"Well, she's wacky about that mayor thing — but other than that she's real nice."

When I got to work, Bertha Jane told me to start right away with Thao.

"I'm going to take a little nap while you're working with Thao, Jason." She brushed a piece of hair from her forehead like she did sometimes. "My stars, I do wish I had more energy but there's just nothing I can do about it."

"Uh-huh." I guessed old people got tired a lot.

"I'll meet you in the garden after my nap, when you're through helping Thao."

"Okay. Is Thao in the den?"

"Yes and I'm sorry there are no cookies today, Jason. I've just been so tired."

"You don't have to make cookies for me."

"I like to, Jason."

"Uh — Bertha Jane?"

"Yes, Jason?"

"They were good — those cookies."

Bertha Jane smiled. "Thank you, dear. Well now, you run along and help Thao."

"Okay."

Thao was sitting in the same place in the den that she was yesterday. Josephine wasn't around today, but Thomas was curled in front of the fireplace.

"Hi, Thao." I smiled.

"Hi, Jason. It nice seeing you at school today."

"I liked seeing you, too." (And I especially liked impressing old Kenny Newman!)

I walked over to the table and sat next to her. She seemed a little tense, but not nearly as much as the day before. I got the paper and pencil ready.

"Should I start asking questions again — or do you want to work on pronouncing what I wrote yesterday?"

"I read paper from yesterday. You help me say things right, okay?"

"Okay." I handed her the paper and Thao began to read. After each sentence, I'd repeat what she said and then she'd say it again after me. Every time her pronunciation got better, I told her it was good. Then she'd smile at me. It always knocked me out. I liked helping her like this. In fact, I felt something I couldn't remember feeling before. Someone needed me.

After we had gone over it several times Thao wanted me to write down the rest of the story. I read over the last part I had written. "We left off where you were in jail for three months. What happened next? After you got out?"

"Okay. It happen like this. Ten month later, my mother have enough money for me to try escape again. It is same as before."

"You mean leaving at dark, traveling for seven hours, and hiding near the river for the boat?"

"Yes, Jason. Same thing. This time I in group with thirty people hidden in house one block from river. In

130

that house they take my bag. No room for it in boat. I take clothes from bag and put them all on. I wear three pants. I take the lemon paste and put in my pocket. There is no talking. At three a.m. we go to river. Boat is there. It is ten yard long and four yard wide. It have motor. We get in quick and we get covered with fishing nets. I cannot breathe. I feel much scared."

"Did you know where you were going?"

"No. Only to ocean. After about three hour more people come from another boat and now we have ninety in this boat."

"You mean ninety?" I wasn't sure I heard the number right, so I wrote it down and showed it to her. "This number?" It was hard to believe so many people were in a small boat. I thought she couldn't mean ninety.

"Yes, that number. We all lie down and waves are so big boat rolls and rolls. It so crowded and hot everyone packed together and getting sick. Sick all over. No food. No water. I chew lemon paste. People go to bathroom in small plastic bag, throw overboard. Sometimes too weak or sick to do that. The whole boat smell terrible. Then after two days, a boat comes over to our boat."

Thao didn't go on. "I think I need a drink of water, Jason." She seemed upset.

"I'll get it for you." I went to the kitchen and brought back a glass of water and handed it to her.

"Thank you." She drank the water and then got up and went to the window and stood looking out for a while. I read over what she had said before I got her the water. In a little while she sat down next to me again.

"Jason, the people from this boat have knife and are bad men. They are thief. We can't understand their speaking. We think they from Thailand. I swallow gold ring."

I was sure Thao had used the wrong word — but I couldn't figure out what she meant. "You mean you hid it somewhere?"

"No. I swallow. In mouth. So it go here." Thao pointed to her stomach. "My mother tell me to do this. Then," her face got bright red, she looked down, "then when go bathroom I get it back."

"Oh." I was embarrassed, too.

"It only money I have. I have to do that."

"Uh-huh." I wasn't sure if I should write that down. I left it out so she wouldn't be embarrassed when she had to read to the class.

"The bad men are on boat two hours. They take everything from everyone. Next day we see sailing boat with about ten people on it. We think it from England. We yell *'CUU CUU!'*"

"What does that mean?"

"It mean 'Help! Help!' This boat throw big cans to us of water and food. We try to steer near cans but waves carry them away."

"You watched cans of water and food just float by you?"

Thao nodded. "We on boat four days with no food, no water. On the fourth day the driver of our boat see

132

land. Everyone is so happy, but we not sure what land it is. We see people on the beach in crowd watching, and we think by the clothes the people wear it is Thailand. As soon as we get close to land everybody jump in water. I can't swim and I choke on salt water. A man from our boat drags me to shore. The people on the shore say 'Thailand! Thailand!' and we can't walk, we fall down on beach."

Josephine had wandered in and Thao picked her up and held her next to her face. "I want my mother to know I am alive. But there is no way to tell her."

I stopped writing. *I want my mother to know I'm alive, too.*

I leaned over and started patting Josephine. It was quiet for a long time.

"Don't be sad, Jason," Thao said finally, looking over at me. "My mother know now. And rest of story better."

"Okay." I picked up the pencil. I wondered if Thao could imagine a mother who lived in the same country — the same city even — who never wanted to see you. But I couldn't picture talking about that to anybody so I just read over the last sentence and started writing as Thao began where we had left off.

"In Thailand, the Thailand police came in a big truck. They give us water and juice. We go in trucks to Leam Sing camp. It is so big with many tents and straw house and many people who escape from Laos and Cambodia, too. About one thousand people live there. It was really hot. One hundred degree every day. Red Cross give the food. I am waiting there hoping to go to America. Some Americans came to the camp. They interview us. We fill out paper they have. They ask how old am I and do I have relative in United States."

"Did you?"

"I have no one. The people who have no relative in America to sponsor them wait for other people to sponsor them like church people. I very *may man*, Jason."

"*May man?*"

"Lucky. It mean, lucky. I was lucky to get sponsor after ten month. Every week list is brought to camp and names of people who can leave are read over loudspeaker. Every week I wait to hear list and hope to hear my name. The people whose names are called get so excited — they yell with happiness. The people who don't hear their name are very sad. Some cry. The day I heard my name on list when they called out 'Thao Nguyen' I couldn't believe it. I was so happy. In camp I wrote many letters to my parents, but I get no letter from them. I don't know if they get my letter. I want so much for them to know I am coming to America. They want that for me more than anything, to come to America.

"On the day we leave we walk up big hill away from camp. Five buses wait. All people who get to leave that day get on buses. Everyone know what country they are going to, some go to France, some to England and America that day. First we go Bangkok. The bus goes to Bangkok airport. We get on airplane.

Many people are on plane, about four hundred people. I know I am going to America, but I don't know where in America I coming. It very long trip. We stop two times. Then come Seattle.

"When we get off plane a worker from a church is there. It is very cold. I am so tired. I don't know anything. I wait there at airport while sponsors for the people in my group come. I so scared I forget every English word I know. I don't know anything. I so afraid. Soon old lady come. It Miss Bertha Jane Fillmore."

Thao waited while I wrote.

"That how I come to America, Jason." She smiled. "I talk better today?"

"You sure did. You were great. I hardly had to ask any questions."

"You good teacher."

"Actually, I was afraid I couldn't do it."

Thao looked puzzled. "You speak and write English — it perfect."

"No, I mean, I'm not so good at talking to people and, uh — I was afraid that, that I wouldn't be able to help you." I couldn't believe I was telling Thao this. But she didn't seem to mind.

"You help very good, Jason. When we practice what you write on paper?"

"Do you want to do it now?"

"I very tired."

"Tomorrow?"

"Yes. That good."

Bertha Jane poked her head in the door of the den. "Are you two about through?" Thomas's tail thumped on the hearth when he heard her voice.

"Uh-huh. Thao wants to work on pronunciation tomorrow."

"All right, then let's get at that garden. What do you say, Jason?"

"Okay." I followed Bertha Jane out to the back yard.

"More weeds, today, dear. We must get rid of them, they're just so destructive. It's not as much fun as planting, of course, but it must be done."

"Okay."

"You know, I used to get very irritable about these weeds and, of course, about lots of life's other little annoyances. But these days I refuse to waste a single second of my time with angry feelings."

"Uh-huh."

I got the tools out of the shed next to the garage and took a little peek through the window at the Bentley. Then I met Bertha Jane in the north end of the yard near some huge evergreen trees.

"Mercy this is a mess! See the blackberry here, Jason?" She pointed to some scraggly bushes all tangled up under the trees.

"Uh-huh."

"They've got to go!"

"Okay."

"A blackberry pie is perfectly lovely once in a while, but if we don't get these out of here they'll take

over the whole yard and we'll be swimming in blackberries."

"Okay."

Bertha Jane picked up some small clippers and a
weed digger and went to a flower bed that was right
next to where I was working on the blackberries. She
was doing something to the roses.

"I love the last roses of autumn."

"Uh-huh."

At the back of the house the windows of the living
room were open and just then I heard all those clocks
inside bonging and dinging and donging and
squawking. It was so weird.

"Time is so precious, Jason. My clocks remind me
of that. You know, dear, death is not the failure of
life, it is part of life. The failure is just not to use time
to grow, to make something as beautiful as possible
out of each moment, to live it to the full." Right after
she said that, Bertha Jane started whipping these
weeds out from around the roses and flinging them
over her shoulder. I guess her nap must have done her
some good because she certainly seemed all revved
up. Weeds were flying everywhere.

"And we can't allow some things to kill other
things. That kind of death is a failure, like these
weeds killing flowers or people killing people."

"Uh-huh." I picked up the shovel. I had to start
digging up the blackberries by the roots, they were
stuck in there so deep.

"Bertha Jane?"

137

"Yes, Jason?"

"Does Thao hear from her parents now?"

"Yes. She certainly does. Word finally got to them from the camp in Thailand. They write letters and each letter takes about twenty days to get here." Bertha Jane took the clippers and cut a few of the roses. "I think I'll put a few of these in a vase," she mumbled. "Don't you think that would be nice, dear?"

"Uh-huh."

"When the mail comes and Thao gets a letter from them, it's a wonderful thing to watch, such joy for her."

I had on these big thick gloves and I grabbed those blackberry bushes and started yanking as hard as I could. Then I don't quite know what happened but I started getting mad. I pulled hell out of those bushes. I was ripping them out of there. I got crazy.

"My stars, Jason, you don't have to —"

"I'm lucky if I hear from my mom once a month and she lives here!" After I blurted that out I really got pissed. I started yanking on the bushes like a maniac.

"Jason?"

"What!"

"I'm starting to tire. Why don't we take a little break, dear."

"Okay," I gasped.

"There's a nice little bench down the path. It's a quiet place to sit overlooking the lake. I think I'd like to sit there and rest a bit."

138

"Okay." I was getting my breath back.

"But I will need a hand getting down the path. My legs are wobblies. Ha-ha, they're on strike!"

Bertha Jane laughed at her joke, which I didn't get, but I laughed politely. She took my arm and I helped her down the path. She was so little and frail, I kind of wondered how she'd pulled out any weeds at all, let alone flung them around.

There was tall grass on either side of the path, which wound around to the right where there was a small stone bench. It looked like it had been carved — the bottoms of the legs had animal feet on them. I held on to Bertha Jane's arm while she sat down.

"Are you okay?" I still held on to her.

"Yes, dear, thank you."

"Okay." I let go and sat next to her.

We just sat there for a while looking out at the lake being quiet. It was real pretty.

Finally Bertha Jane said, "What I love about this, Jason, is that it's completely different than television."

"Different than television?"

"Yes. You see when you look out over the lake you never quite know what color it will be or how the clouds will be that day. It's always changing. Each day the universe has some new surprise and we never know just what it will be. But on television, you just look in the paper and it tells you — seven a.m. news, eight a.m. aerobics."

"My mom used to watch that."

"Did she?"

"Yeah, when she lived with us. She moved out last spring. It's just me and Dad there now and he's never home."

"I see."

"I don't like it much."

"No, I would think not."

"I tried to talk to my dad last night, but he just wanted to change the subject."

"How often that happens. It's so difficult sometimes just to get a person to listen."

"I know and that's all I wanted him to do — no big deal or anything."

"Oh, Jason," Bertha Jane started unscrewing the top of her cane. "I'm afraid it is a big deal or else more people would know how to do it."

"I never thought listening was that hard. Talking is what's hard for me. I've probably talked more here than I ever have in my life — and I haven't said that much."

"Well listening is terribly hard. You mustn't underestimate it. In fact, it's so important that I always keep this little poem with me right here in the file." She turned her cane upside down and shook out this rolled-up piece of paper. "Shall I read it to you?" she asked.

"Okay." (You're too old for this, Kovak.)

I felt kind of funny sitting there while Bertha Jane read to me. It reminded me of when I was a little kid and Mom read me stories — but I liked it.

This is what Bertha Jane read:

When I ask you to listen to me and you change the subject, I feel I am alone.

When I ask you to listen to me and you start giving advice, you have not done what I asked.

When I ask you to listen to me and you begin to tell me why I shouldn't feel that way, you are trampling on my feelings.

When I ask you to listen to me and you feel you have to do something to solve my problem, you have failed me, strange as that may seem.

Listen! All I asked was that you listen, not talk or do — just hear me.

Advice is cheap: twenty-five cents will get you both Dear Abby and Billy Graham in the same newspaper.

All I can I do for myself. I am not helpless. Maybe discouraged and faltering but not helpless.

When you do something for me that I can and need to do for myself, you contribute to my fear and inadequacy.

But, when you accept as a simple fact that I do feel what I feel, no matter how distressful, then I can get about the business of understanding what's behind this feeling.

Now, more than ever, I need to talk.

And, I will listen to you. It will go much better for us. We will be closer.

Anon. Cancer Patient

After she was through reading she handed it to me. "Can I keep this?"

"Yes, dear. I have other copies. That's just my file copy."

"Thanks. Who's Anon?"

"That means anonymous, dear. The author wanted to remain unknown."

"I wish my dad knew about this poem."

"Perhaps you could give it to him someday."

"Oh, he'd never get it. He'd see at the bottom that it was written by a sick person and he'd think it didn't have anything to do with him."

"Oh, Jason. We are all dying; the difference between us is only in the length and quality of the time that is left. And as long as any one of us has a brain that works we can change and grow. Even your father. I'm sure of that."

"Well, he does try to help me, but he just says I should stand in front of the mirror and say a bunch of shit — oops. I'm sorry, Miss Fill — I mean Bertha Jane." I felt my face get all red.

Bertha Jane brushed her hair off her forehead. "I have always been of the opinion that the true obscenities, Jason, are the words that are used to degrade a person of a particular race, nationality, or religion. All the rest of it — like the word 'shit,' for instance, are just bathroom words, or words that refer to parts of the human anatomy, or sexual activity which results in the birth of human beings. These words can apply to anyone in the world and, therefore, although they may not always be pleasant words, I for one do not consider them obscene."

"Oh." (I couldn't believe I was sitting on this bench with an old lady who just said "shit" and then "sexual activity" — it was so bizarre. I wondered if she would think my ideas about sexual activity with me and Lisa LaRue were obscene — but I sure wasn't going to tell her about that! I bet if people knew how often I thought about that stuff they'd think I was a real pervert.)

"Jason, do you think I preach too much?"

"Preach?"

"Yes. My brother, Harry, always accused me of preaching. I suppose I do have quite a few opinions on things, but at my age maybe I've earned the right to preach a bit. What do you think?" Her eyes twinkled.

"I wish my mom cared enough to preach to me. I think what you say is very nice."

We kept sitting on the bench like that talking about a lot of stuff. I liked being there. I told Bertha Jane how I couldn't talk to people. And I told her how Kenny Newman was always with Stephanie, and Dad was with those ladies, and Mom was with Roger Albright and how Dad calls him That Fruitcake, and about my job at Wendy's and the robbery and how I thought I was going to die, and about being a wimp.

"A wimp?"

"Kind of a coward."

"Hmm. Well, Jason, it seems to me that when everyone you care about seems to be gone, it takes a lot of courage just to remain cheerful and keep going."

"But it really got me about Thao — leaving her parents and all that stuff she went through." I picked up some sticks from the ground by the feet of the bench and started breaking them. "I felt stupid for getting upset that my mom left. I mean, it's not such a big deal like what happened to Thao."

"Jason, on the surface it appears Thao has no family, but the bonds with her family are strong and their sacrifice for her was great. In fact she suffers guilt sometimes at their sacrifice for her and she worries constantly about them."

"That's what I mean. Compared to that it seems dumb to me that I get upset about Mom not wanting to see me and Dad being gone all the time."

"Jason, it seems to me that you suffer the pain of repeated rejection. It is not the same kind of pain that Thao has, but I doubt it is any less. She can reassure herself about how deeply her parents care for her, and that's something I get the impression you're not very sure of. In fact, I imagine it hurts a great deal."

"Oh."

Then I heard all the clocks again, all bonging and donging and dinging and squawking. It was time for me to go. Those clocks didn't sound as weird as they usually did. I guess I was just getting used to them.

I felt pretty happy driving home from Bertha Jane's house. I was doing my favorite thing, which was (of course) thinking about Lisa LaRue. I was starting to count the days until I would get to drive Bertha Jane to the doctor in the Bentley and then go to be with the dark-eyed beauty in the flesh (ha). While I was stopped at the traffic light where there is a cleaner's on the corner, I looked up and saw the sign they have on top of the cleaner's. On one side it said:

LET'S BE CLOTHES FRIENDS

on the other side it said:

DROP PANTS HERE FOR FAST SERVICE

(Ha!)

CHAPTER 11

THE night before I was supposed to meet Lisa LaRue I was a nervous wreck. I had counted the days all right, and now that I was going to really meet her I was scared. I decided the only way to mellow out would be to practice for the occasion.

I spent a lot of time trying on the hat I had bought at the army-navy surplus place. I hoped it looked like a driver's hat — it did, sort of (I think). First I'd push it back on my head and then I'd try it cocked over one eye. Then I tried to make sexy faces in the mirror. What the hell — why not? My dad gets up every morning and says all that crap to himself looking at his own face in the mirror. I figured what I was doing wasn't any stupider than that.

I also spent a lot of time that night trying to figure out what it meant to be gentle and devilish. I just wasn't sure how I was supposed to be gentle and how

146

I was supposed to be devilish. And what was devilish anyway? I mean Lisa LaRue's letter didn't sound like she was into some kind of kinky stuff. I read some of the *How to Fascinate Women* book.

Finally I decided that gentle meant I would tenderly touch her face with my fingertips and devilish would be that I would suddenly lift her in my arms and throw her on the bed (I hoped she didn't weigh too much more than my Joe Weider Weight Set). I wasn't exactly sure how we would get into this bedroom, but since she was an older woman, I figured she would know about that part. Besides, I wouldn't have to worry about that until the second date. Maybe I could find more books, although when I looked through *The Joy of Sex* at the bookstore, I'd noticed it didn't have a chapter on underwear removal. I'd have to figure that out later. Tomorrow, I would just have to act gentle and devilish while we were in the bar. I would gently cover her hand with mine and then I would devilishly grab her leg under the table (ha! — she'd love it!).

Friday morning in homeroom we were supposed to fill out information forms for the attendance office. I was thinking so much about Lisa LaRue I almost forgot my own address! I also just stared at the blank where it said, "Nearest friend or relative in case of emergency." I wasn't sure who to put. I thought about it for a long time. Finally, I wrote in, "Bertha Jane Fillmore." It was strange. Even though I worked for her and had only known her for a little while, she seemed like my nearest friend.

Bertha Jane was all ready to go when I got to her house after school. She had on this nice little dress and a little hat too, she looked kind of dressed up. I had on black slacks and a white shirt and I was carrying the driver hat.

"This is so I'll look like a real driver," I told Bertha Jane.

"Oh, that's very nice, Jason." Bertha Jane smiled and her face crinkled up. "Well, let's be off."

I followed her out to the garage and she opened her purse and handed me the keys to the Bentley. "Here you are, Jason."

"Thanks."

I opened the back door for her, but she didn't get in.

"Jason, I think I'd prefer sitting right next to you in the front seat."

"Oh, okay." I opened the front door and helped her in.

"Thank you, dear."

Then I went around the back of the car and got in the driver's side. What a fantastic car! And it was in practically perfect condition, too.

"Bertha Jane? Would it be all right if we drove around the block a few times, just so I could get the feel of the car, before we head out into traffic?"

"That would be fine, dear. I'll open the garage door."

"Oh no Miss Fill — I mean, Bertha Jane, I'll do that." I opened the car door and started to jump out.

"I can do it, Jason. I have the magic." Then she

148

chuckled and whipped an automatic garage door opener out of her purse. "I just love to do this," she said as she stuck her arm straight out in front of her and pushed the button. "I consider most mechanical things my natural enemies, but this little gadget here is one I do rather like."

I headed the car slowly out of the garage and then Bertha Jane flung her arm over her shoulder and pushed the button again and the garage door closed behind us. She chuckled as it went down.

I drove slowly around the block. The car handled like a dream. I wished Kenny or the other guys I hang around with at school, Chris Weber or Dave Horowitz, could see me now. I'd just love to roll by and give a little wave and say "Hi, guys," real casual like.

"You seem to be driving it very well, Jason."

"Thanks. It's a wonderful car, Bertha Jane."

"Well, if you feel ready, then I suspect we'd best be on our way."

"Okay. Uh — where is the doctor's office?"

"Oh, it's my forgettery again!" Bertha Jane laughed. "It's at the Mason Clinic, Jason, Ninth and Terry."

"Okay." I headed the car out of the neighborhood and onto Rainier Avenue. I kept hoping I might see someone I knew, but I didn't want to look around too much — I wanted to drive really safe and everything. The last thing I wanted was to bump into something with that Bentley and hurt Bertha Jane or the car.

I got to the Mason Clinic and pulled up in front.

Then I jumped out of the car and ran around and opened the door for her. I held her arm and helped her get out. The Bentley was pretty high off the ground and I had to kind of lift her down, she was so little.

On the sidewalk, she adjusted her little hat. "Well, Jason, you run along now and use the car as you wish. I'll meet you right here at five thirty."

"Uh — do you need any help getting to the office or anything?"

"No, dear. I can get there by myself just fine."

"Okay. See you at five thirty."

Then she waved and turned and walked into the clinic. I wondered why she had to go to the doctor so much. I guessed it was just being old. Old people seem to go to the doctor a lot.

I drove down Madison toward downtown and the SeaFirst Building. I knew right where I was going because I had scoped the whole thing out in my car a zillion times, getting ready for this day.

I drove into the garage of the SeaFirst Building and stopped at the window where the guy gives out the ticket.

"That's a real beauty — a Bentley, right?"

"Yep."

"What year?'

"Nineteen thirty-nine." I grinned and tipped my hat.

The guy whistled. Then he gave me the ticket and I drove into the garage and parked the car. I locked it, put the keys in my pocket, and walked over to the elevator. I got out on the main floor of the building and then I went to the elevator, an express to the top floor, where the Mirabeau restaurant was. I held on to the hat real tight, and all the way up on the elevator I kept practicing over and over what I had planned to say. My heart was thumping as much as it had during the robbery at Wendy's.

The elevator doors opened on the top floor and I got out behind a bunch of businessmen in suits and a few business ladies, too. I saw the sign for the Mirabeau — it was really fancy. There was a guy at the front desk wearing a dark blue suit. I walked up to him. My knees were shaking. I cleared my throat, hoping my voice would come out really deep.

"Pardon me —"

"Can I help you, sir?" The guy had a French accent.

"Yes. I am the driver for Mr. T. Worthington Jones and I need to deliver a message from him to someone waiting in the lounge."

"Right that way, sir." The guy pointed to his left.

"Thank you." I took a deep breath — so far so good. I had been really worried about getting carded, but that didn't happen, thank God. I guess fancy places like the Mirabeau don't have to worry much about kids under twenty-one trying to sneak in. Probably no one under twenty-one has those kind of bucks. And now I was really just walking right on into the bar — I had really gotten past the guy at the

151

door! I had practiced this whole thing so many times and now it was really working — it was really all coming true!

I stood near the door to the bar. It wasn't real bright in there and I squinted and looked around. There were business people everywhere and some tables with men and women and then some tables with just women. I kept looking for a lady all by herself in a red dress. I twirled the hat around in my hands. I was getting extremely nervous. I was so nervous, I was thinking about leaving — *then I saw her.*

It had to be her. She was the only lady sitting by herself in the whole place and she had on a red dress. It was Lisa LaRue. She was a real person! I cleared my throat and walked over to where she was sitting at this table by the window. I walked up to the table.

"Miss LaRue?"

"Yes?"

"— Whoops —" My foot caught on the chair across from her. I tripped and fell into the stupid table.

"Watch out!"

"I'm uh — I'm terribly sorry."

"Who the hell are you?" She sounded really pissed.

"Uh — I am the driver for Mr. T. Worthington Jones," I mumbled.

"Oh," she said, sounding quite cheerful all of a sudden. "Isn't that nice." She talked in this breathless voice — she was now very enthusiastic.

"Uh — my name is Jason Kovak and I — uh — have a message for you from Mr. Jones."

"Hi there, Jason." She stuck her hand out. It had long purple fingernails on it. "I'm Lisa." We shook hands and then she said, "Would you like to sit down?"

"Uh — okay — thanks." I fumbled around trying to get a good hold on the stupid chair and then I sat down. As soon as I did, this cocktail waitress in a little outfit appeared at the table.

"What can I get for you, sir?" she asked.

It was hard not to stare at her. There wasn't a whole lot to her outfit and she had these long beautiful legs. I tried to keep my eyes on her face.

"I'll just have a Coke." Then I said to Lisa LaRue, "I can't drink when I'm on duty." (This was one of the lines I had practiced.)

"Oh yes, of course."

My eyes started adjusting to the light and I was able to really look at Lisa LaRue. She looked like she was around thirty or so and she had dark eyes with a lot of gooey stuff on them. She had longish brownish hair and it looked like it had some gooey stuff in it or something because it stuck out a lot and looked kind of wild. The body in the red dress was amazing. I had to concentrate to look at her face just like with the waitress. I wished I had practiced face looking. It got embarrassing when my eyes wouldn't stay there.

"Umm, Jason — it is Jason, isn't it?"

"Uh-huh."

"You mentioned you had a message from Mr. Jones?"

"Right. He sent me here to find you. He's terribly

153

sorry, but he's not able to make it today. He came down with the flu, the Himalayan flu — it sometimes strikes people after they've come back from the climb and he's so sick with it, he can hardly talk. That's why he didn't call you and he sent me in person."

"Oh. That's too bad." She sounded really disappointed.

The waitress brought my Coke and I checked out her legs again. I couldn't help it. They were all bare, right in front of my face.

"How long does this kind of flu usually last?" She sipped on her glass of wine.

"Usually just a few weeks."

"Well ..." she smiled and the tip of her tongue touched her front teeth, "maybe T.W. and I can get together as soon as he's all better."

"Well, that's just the problem. In a few weeks he has to leave immediately for New Zealand."

"Oh."

I cleared my throat. "He did mention to me that perhaps I could make you happy." (I said it without stuttering — it came out great, just like I had practiced.)

"Huh?"

"Yes, you see —" Just as I said this, some spit flew out of my mouth and hit her in the face. I looked out the window while she wiped it off with a napkin.

I didn't know what to do. How could I fix this up? Then I saw a flower in a vase on the table. *How to Fascinate Women* said all women love flowers. I would take it out of the vase, hand it to her and say, "Lisa, you are more beautiful than this lovely flower."

I put the hat on and cocked it over one eye. "Lisa, you are more beautiful than this —" As I tried to pull out the flower the vase dumped over.

"Oh, for God's sake!" She stood up, wiped her dress — water was all over her — and then she threw her napkin down on the table. "Tell your Mr. T. Worthington Jones that the next time he has a message for me he better deliver it himself!"

CHAPTER 12

"I HOPE you didn't get too bored while I was at the doctor's, Jason." Bertha Jane held my arm as I lifted her up into the car.

"Oh no." (Ha.)

"Good."

Bertha Jane's eyes kept closing and her head would nod as I drove her home. We didn't talk much. I was glad, too, because I didn't feel like talking after what happened with me and Lisa LaRue.

Right after she yelled at me that the next time T. Worthington Jones had a message to deliver he should deliver it himself, she stomped out. I just sat there in the bar like a wimp, sipping my Coke. God, what a disaster. The only thing that cheered me up was looking at the legs of the cocktail waitress.

I couldn't believe what had happened with Lisa

LaRue after all my wonderful plans. It made me sick. If just one thing had gone wrong — like only falling into the stupid table, if that had been the only thing I messed up on — maybe I could have recovered. But spitting on her and then dumping water in her lap — it was disgusting to think about it.

But I told myself I would just have to forget it. There was no question I was all through with Lisa LaRue. But then I started to wonder — was I really finished forever? If the first time a guy gets up to bat and he strikes out, does that mean he should just up and quit the game? As I thought about this, I realized that there really wasn't anything stopping me from trying to answer another ad from the *Weekly*. There are zillions of these wonderful women out there advertising each week and now that I had the shakes out of my system, maybe I'd be more confident the next time. What the hell, if I kept trying I just might get to first base! (Ha!) I convinced myself I should just put that whole mess with Lisa LaRue behind me and try again. I had survived it, hadn't I? I didn't die from being such a jerk, so I might as well give the whole thing another shot. It couldn't possibly turn out to be as sickening as that mess with Lisa LaRue.

I was thinking about this, trying to psych myself up as I pulled into the driveway to Bertha Jane's house. I drove around the curving driveway and parked in front of the garage. I looked over at Bertha Jane. She was sound asleep.

I put my hand on her shoulder. I was real gentle. I

hoped she was okay and not sick or anything. Maybe she just needed lots of check-ups, like an old car that needs to be tuned up frequently.

"Bertha Jane," I whispered.

Slowly she opened her eyes.

"We're home."

"Oh my stars, Jason. I fell right asleep." She fumbled through her purse for the garage door opener. When she found it, she handed it to me. "Could you do it, dear?"

I took the opener and pushed the button. The door went up and I drove the car in. Then I handed the opener back to Bertha Jane.

"I feel a little weak and my tummy has some problems after I go to the doctor, Jason. I have some medicine to take for it and then I should be fine. But I need a little nap first."

I helped her out of the car. I was glad she had medicine for whatever it was. "Uh — Bertha Jane?"

"Yes, Jason."

"Is there anything you'd like me to do now?"

"Well, Thao is making some yard signs. Perhaps you could help her."

"Yard signs?"

"For the campaign."

"Oh, okay." I guessed she meant about her campaign for mayor. She hadn't talked about it that much and I still wasn't sure if she really was running for mayor or what. Bertha Jane didn't seem nuts to me anymore, but I still had to admit this mayor thing was pretty loony. I followed her into the house and she said Thao was working on the yard signs in the ballroom and that I could find her there. Then she said she'd be down after her tummy got settled and after she'd had her little nap.

She never had given me a tour of the house, so I had to wander around and figure out where the ballroom was. The house was huge. I bet it had over twenty-five rooms in it.

The fact that the old house had a room named the ballroom was pretty amazing. It made me think about dances and stuff and then I thought about the Homecoming dance coming up. I hadn't thought about my finking out on Karen Jacobsen in a long time. She talked to me in homeroom but I still choked and never could think of anything to say back. Maybe I'd never be able to talk to a girl. Then I thought about Thao. She was a girl. I could ask her.

"But what if I throw up again?"

"But you can talk to Thao."

"Maybe she just talks to me because she has to."

"She's beautiful. Just ask her, dummy."

"What if she says no?"

"Don't be a wimp."

"I'll ask her some other day."

"Do it today."

"It's not a big deal. I can do it — later."

"Why not now?"

"I have to wait for the right time."

"He who hesitates is lost."

"When in doubt — don't."

It went on like this with me wandering around the

house trying to find the ballroom, arguing with myself — Loony Tune Time all over again.

I went up some stairs in the pantry off the kitchen. It was a good guess, because after three flights, when I opened the door at the top of the stairs, I was in a huge room. It had to be the ballroom. Thao was there with big pieces of white cardboard laid out all over the floor.

"Hi, Thao."

She looked up and smiled. "Hi, Jason."

That smile of hers always knocked me out. I stood in the doorway, watching her and arguing with myself.

"Jason?"

"Huh?"

"Does Bertha Jane need me?"

"Oh, no, she wanted me to help you with the yard signs." I walked over to where Thao was sitting on the floor.

"Okay. I show you." Thao had a stencil and a few cans of orange enamel spray paint. She held up one of the signs she had finished. It said BERTHA JANE FILLMORE FOR MAYOR.

"That looks nice, Thao. You did a good job." I talked too fast and Thao didn't understand what I said, so I had to slow down and say it again. She gave me this big smile after I said it the second time. It knocked me out all over again.

I sat down next to her and started working. There were only six pieces of cardboard. I guess Bertha Jane's campaign didn't include a big media blitz. But

I kind of wondered if this was the whole thing. It seemed so nutty to be making these signs, but I guess at that point I'd have done just about anything to make Bertha Jane happy.

As I sprayed my sign I started talking to myself again.

"Just ask her now, dummy."

"I can't just blurt it out."

"Well then strike up a little conversation first."

"Okay, okay — I'll do it."

I sat there on the floor spraying my sign, trying to think of some conversation. I decided to ask her about school.

"Do you like Ingraham, Thao?" I asked real slowly.

"It okay, but very hard to understand what happening there."

"It must have seemed strange at first."

"Yes. Really strange. Like first thing I see what everybody wearing. It so strange."

"What did you wear to school in Viet Nam?"

"Dresses, long white dresses. All the girls wear that. I really miss those dresses." She looked kind of sad.

"What do the guys wear?"

"Always they wear blue pant and white shirt. All look the same, very nice."

I thought about some of the people at school with purple, orange, and blue hair sticking straight up with gooey crap on it, wearing ripped-up-on-purpose clothes and guys wearing earrings. She must have thought she'd landed on another planet.

"Thao — uh — at school they're having this, um, dance. Maybe you saw the signs in the halls about it like this," I pointed to the signs. Thao looked very confused. "You know a dance, like music, dancing, MTV." Thao looked even more confused. I decided to start over again. "Thao, do you know the word music?"

"Yes, I know that word."

"Okay. Good. Uh — do you know the word dance?" I started humming and pretending I was dancing. The whole thing was kind of like playing charades.

"Oh yes, dance with music. I know that." Thao smiled.

"Thao, at school, at night, the people come on Saturday night and they have music and the people dance." (They also get stoned and drunk and throw up in the bathrooms but I didn't mention that.)

"Yes, I hear about that."

"Well, Thao — would you like to come with me to school for this music and dancing?" I asked real slowly. (I couldn't believe I was really asking her.)

Thao didn't say anything, so I asked her again even more slowly this time. She just looked down at the sign. She was real quiet.

When she finally looked up at me her face was sort of flushed, she looked upset and her eyes were shiny. "Jason. I can't go."

"Oh." My stomach turned over — I wanted to crawl under one of the signs.

"I feel an attack inside."

"Okay," I mumbled, feeling like a total nerd.

I had no idea what Thao was talking about. I mean, I didn't know if she was sick or something or what that meant. Did she think I'd attack her? I felt really bad. I started talking to myself again.

"You never should have asked her, dummy."

"I tried, didn't I?"

"You blew it."

"Nothing ventured — nothing gained."

"Oh, shut up!"

I didn't say anything more to Thao, I just kept working on the signs. She didn't say anything either. It was sort of tense and I tried to concentrate on the signs. I just wanted to forget the whole thing.

When we had finished all six signs we took them downstairs. Bertha Jane was up from her nap and was in the kitchen when we walked in with the signs. Thao and I each held one up.

"Oh," Bertha Jane clapped her hands together, "they're lovely!" She was so excited — it made me feel a little better, even if I did think the mayor thing was bizarre.

"Jason," Bertha Jane said, going over to the pile of signs, "I think we should stack them in the garage for now and then tomorrow we can distribute them."

"Okay." I took the signs out to the garage and leaned them up against the side wall next to the firewood.

While I was putting the signs away, I noticed that

it seemed to be getting cold all of a sudden. I looked out the garage window. The sky was dark. Wind was whipping the branches of the trees all over the place and leaves were swirling everywhere. It was spooky.

I finished stacking the signs and went back in the house. As I closed the door behind me, a big gust of wind blew against it, slamming it hard. It was nice to be in the kitchen — it was so bright and cheery. Thao and Bertha Jane were sitting at the kitchen table in front of big windows that looked out over the back yard and the lake. The lake looked dark and choppy in the light from the Mercer Island bridge and the trees were bent over from the wind — the branches on some of them looked like they might break right off.

As I went over to Thao and Bertha Jane, a big flash of lightning streaked over the lake. Thunder cracked. Bertha Jane and I jumped when we heard it, but Thao screamed. It scared me to hear her scream like that. I didn't know what was happening. Then she started to shake, her whole body just shaking and shaking. The lightning flashed again and then another thunderous crack. Everything went dark.

"Jason," Bertha Jane stood up, "the power must be out. I'll get some candles. You must hold Thao's hand and talk to her the whole time through this storm. Just keep talking."

It was really dark. I felt my way around the table and sat next to Thao. I reached for her hand. It was so cold, it was like she was dead only she was trembling all over the place — it was like her whole body

164

was a washing machine that had too many clothes in it.

"Thao, it's just a storm in the sky — a thunderstorm and there's nothing to be afraid of." I put my arm around her. "I'm here and Bertha Jane is here and Josephine is here and Thomas is here and Bertha Jane is going to find some candles and today we made such pretty signs and I thought your signs were better than mine and I liked hearing about the white dresses that you used to wear to school and it sounded real nice and I bet you would look real pretty in those dresses and very soon the storm will be over and everything will be all right and then maybe we can have some of those nice chocolate chip cookies and tomorrow when it's nice out you can come out to the garden and see how we're making it look better and it will be a happy day and don't worry now because the storm won't hurt you and I'm here and Bertha Jane's here . . ." I just babbled on and on like that but Thao would start to scream every time the thunder cracked and then she'd shake and shake. Then she'd seem to hear me and get a little calmer until the next crack of thunder. Then it would start all over again.

I saw a light glowing across the kitchen. "Here we are," Bertha Jane said, as she came in carrying a candle. The rain pounded away against the windows and the lightning and thunder seemed to have stopped. Bertha Jane put the candle in the middle of the table. Then she got some candlesticks out of the cupboards and stuck candles in them and put them all over the place. It was kind of beautiful, everything all glowing

165

with candles everywhere. I could feel Thao begin to stop shaking so I let go of her and went around to the other side of the table.

"Jason?" Thao looked up at me.

"Huh?"

"Thank you," she said softly.

"Sure." She was so little and so scared, I just wanted to hold her some more.

Then I had a funny feeling inside. When I had held her, I had talked. I had talked and talked and talked.

CHAPTER 13

I HELPED Bertha Jane into the Bentley. She had another doctor's appointment and this time, because I was still feeling a bit blown away after my disaster with Lisa LaRue, I hadn't gotten up the nerve to make any more plans of my own to keep me busy while I waited for Bertha Jane. I had brought the *Weekly* though (never being one to entirely give up — ha!). I thought it would give me something to do while I sat in the car all that time.

It was raining as I headed the Bentley out the driveway. All the leaves were gone from the trees now and it was getting colder. Driving down Mountain-view Avenue, I noticed the Wendy's where I used to work. Had it only been a month since I quit? I looked over at Bertha Jane. It still seemed strange to me that I hadn't been working for her that long. I felt like I had known her my whole life. She was all dressed up again in her nice little dress and the same little hat she had been wearing all the time lately. As I headed down McClellan Street toward Rainier Avenue, I turned on the windshield wipers. There was just a quiet rain — not like before when we'd had that big storm.

"Bertha Jane?"

"Yes, Jason."

"When we had that thunderstorm and Thao got so scared — well, I just wondered about that."

"Bombs."

"Bombs?"

"Yes, when she was a child, in fact most of her young life, there were bombs. Houses, people, friends, loved ones . . . everywhere around her there was terrible destruction."

"Thunder sounds like bombs to her?"

"Yes."

"Bertha Jane?"

"Yes, Jason."

"I asked her to a dance at school and she seemed to get real upset. She said no and she said she felt an attack inside. I didn't know what she meant."

"Well, I think that was probably because in Viet Nam, Jason, at her age, girls don't date the way they do here. In fact, sometimes marriages are still arranged by the families. But at the very least the parents must know the boy and his family very well in order to allow a young girl to spend time with him."

"But her parents aren't here — I mean, it's different here."

"Jason, when Thao says she feels an attack inside, I think she means it is like a war going on inside of her. I'm sure part of her really wanted to go to the dance with you, but the other part knows her parents wouldn't approve and so she was at war within herself."

"Oh." It made sense the way Bertha Jane explained it. But I felt sad.

"You see, dear, one of the ways she can still feel a sense of family and feel close to them is to only behave in ways that they would like. If Thao did things they wouldn't approve of it would seem to her like she was betraying them."

"Oh."

"You do see, don't you?"

"I guess so."

"But, Jason dear, even if you and Thao can't have a romantic relationship, you can be friends."

"Well, I just asked her like a friend — I mean, it wasn't any big deal or anything."

Bertha Jane folded her hands in her lap, "You and Thao may be lucky, you may truly be friends, and that is an unusual thing between a young man and a young woman. To know true friendship at this age is a great gift."

She looked up at me and brushed some hair off her forehead. "I'm not against sex, Jason, but sometimes when things are felt with lust and passion, true friendship can be obscured. To know a friendship at this age can be quite a precious thing. I'm afraid that sex often changes and confuses things. Sometimes the desire for fusion of the flesh can overwhelm us and make true meeting of the souls impossible."

"Uh-huh." Here we were again, me and Bertha Jane talking about all this stuff, and here I sat with the *Weekly* tucked under the front seat, gearing up to send in for more women. It was embarrassing.

"Sex is easy, Jason. It's love that is the struggle. And with a true friendship you can learn about the nature of each other, about the nature of a young male and a young female. I for one think they're quite different."

"Uh-huh." I turned the corner onto Rainier Avenue. I wondered what she meant about sex being easy. It sure wasn't easy for me. I remembered all over again that mess with me and Lisa LaRue. Easy? (Ha!)

"I think we must be careful when we speak of the differences between male and female, Jason. Different doesn't mean unequal, only different. The different sexes have different strengths and we can learn from each other. Don't you think?"

"I guess so."

"And think of this, Jason. There was one American Indian tribe that avoided unnecessary combat by giving the war-making decision to their women because they knew women would fight for survival but not for 'honor.'"

"Yeah, but doesn't that just show that men are worse than women?"

"Ah, but Jason, dear, it was the men who recognized this about the women and made that decision.

170

To recognize limitations and to transcend them for the good of all — that is wisdom!"

"Oh." I turned left on Terry and drove to the front of the Mason Clinic.

"Well, here we are again. I suppose I've been preaching again."

"I like to hear you talk." I smiled at her.

"Thank you, dear. I'll see you in a little while, Jason."

"Okay." I got out of the car and went around and helped Bertha Jane down. She headed for the door and then turned and gave me a little wave before she went in. I wondered what they did to her in there.

I parked the car and then I just sat there. I was thinking about all that stuff she had said, trying to figure it out. I especially wondered what she meant about sex being easy and love being the struggle. But I couldn't keep my mind on it. Instead, I kept thinking about the *Weekly* stuck under the front seat, and I couldn't help wanting to try the whole thing again. It seemed to me that I could think about friendship and love and all that stuff Bertha Jane had said once I, too, found out that sex was easy. Yes, I would like to find that out. I pulled out the *Weekly* from under the seat and started reading the ads.

After carefully reading every ad in the whole newspaper I settled on three that I thought were pretty good possibilities. Actually, they were the only three that didn't say what age man they wanted:

NOT LUCKY, WANT A STRIKE? How about some champagne and moonlight

bowling? Fun, outgoing woman will demon-
strate how to have a good time! Reply PO
Box 9016, Seattle 98112.

ATTRACTIVE, CUDDLY WOMAN
wants to create warm and loving, playful
and supportive, intimate relationship with
man desiring same. Unwilling to limit possibilities with particulars just yet. Let's talk.
Reply PO Box 9022, Seattle 98105.

CAN AFFORD only small ad: Woman
seeks man for cheap thrills. Reply PO Box
9039, Seattle 98122.

It seemed to me that I should only pick one of these
to answer. I was practically positive it would have to
turn out better than that disaster with Lisa LaRue,
now that I had a little practice under my belt. But
just in case I did mess up again, I thought I really
should take it more slowly.

But which one? The lady bowler, the cuddly
woman, or cheap thrills? This was a very tough decision. I gave this a great deal of thought for about a
minute or two — then, like any normal guy, I decided on cheap thrills.

When I saw Bertha Jane coming out of the clinic, I
stuck the newspaper back under the seat and got out
of the car to help her get in.

"Thank you, dear."

"Sure." I got in on the driver's side. When I looked
over at Bertha Jane, I saw her eyes beginning to close.
She sure got tired after going to that doctor. I was

beginning to get worried about her. As I drove away from the clinic, she opened them a minute.

"Jason, I'm going to take my tummy medicine and have a little nap when we get home." She unscrewed the top of her cane, pulled out a piece of paper and handed it to me. "And while I'm taking my nap, I'd like you to get about a hundred copies of this made at a Copy Mart. This is my campaign literature, Jason. There's a candidates' meeting at the Mt. Baker Community Club and I must be there to make a speech. I'd like you to drive me there and stay to hand the fliers out to people."

"Okay." So, *she was actually serious about running for mayor.* I had never quite believed it before — but I'd be the last person to tell her it was crazy.

"Bertha Jane?"

"Yes, Jason." She seemed hardly able to keep her eyes open.

"Would it be okay if I used your typewriter for a few minutes before I go to the Copy Mart?"

"Of course, dear."

"Thanks."

It was nice not to have to lie to Bertha Jane and tell her I was doing something for school, like I did with Mom. Bertha Jane's so nice, she didn't even ask why I needed to use it.

When we got to her house, she took a nap and I went to the room off the kitchen where she kept the typewriter and a lot of stuff for the campaign. I read the ad from the *Weekly* one more time. "CAN AF-

FORD only small ad: Woman seeks man for cheap thrills. Reply PO Box 9039, Seattle 98122." Then I typed up this letter to "Cheap Thrills."

> *Dear woman with the small ad,*
> *What a clever ad you placed in the personal column of the* Weekly. *I was so impressed with your ability to be so exact and enticing all at the same time. I will be in Seattle next week to visit some of the wineries in the Northwest, as I am on my way to my home in New Zealand after making a tour of the wine country of France. My private jet will be landing at Boeing Field early in the week. It has been a stimulating and useful business trip for me and I know it will benefit the millions of acres of grapes and the huge wineries I own in New Zealand. I would love a little fun on my stopover in Seattle and your ad seemed to indicate a fine sense of fun on your part. I hope you would like to get together during my layover in Seattle. I can be reached through PO Box 963, Seattle, WA 98144*
>

Yours very truly,
T. Worthington Jones

Layover in Seattle (ha!). I couldn't wait to send this letter. I mailed it on my way to the Copy Mart. I had to wait there a long time while they made copies of the flier. When I got back to the house, Bertha Jane was up from her nap. Thao had made some sandwiches and after we ate them it was time to go to the candidates' thing. Bertha Jane had on her nice

174

little dress and her little hat, and she was wearing a flower from the garden.

"How do I look, Jason?"

"Real nice, Bertha Jane."

"I thought the flower would be a nice touch, don't you think?"

"Yes, it's very pretty."

"Well, I guess the time has come." Bertha Jane smiled and patted her hair.

I had never been to anything like candidates' night before and I didn't know quite what to expect. Thao wanted to go too, so the three of us got into the Bentley and we were on our way.

Thao sat in the back seat holding the fliers and Bertha Jane sat next to me kind of mumbling to herself, practicing her speech. She had been working really hard on it.

She stopped mumbling and looked over at me. "You know, Jason, I do hope to clear the Fillmore name a bit with all of this, too."

"Uh-huh."

"You see it's not that Millard did anything criminal. It's just that he really didn't do anything much at all. And the little he did do — supporting the Compromise of 1850 — was something I don't approve of at all. Millard believed that the Union could only be kept together by allowing the South to have some of the things it wanted. That compromise was a law that required people to help slave-owners get back their runaway slaves. Of course, no one remembers that, but I think it was dreadful. He was never elected, you know. He was vice-president and he just got to be president because President Zachary Taylor died."

"No, I didn't know."

"Not many people do. But you see, the main thing I don't want to be is mediocre. I believe I have an important message and I just hope the people will notice that."

"Uh-huh." It was almost 7:30. I stopped the Bentley in front of the Mt. Baker Community Club and helped Bertha Jane get out of the car.

"Jason, dear, you park the car and Thao and I will meet you inside."

"Okay."

I found a parking space on Mt. Rainier Drive, not far from the community club. When I went in, there were a lot of people milling around — the thing hadn't started yet. A big coffee pot was set up in the back of the room and people were getting coffee in Styrofoam cups and standing around talking. Bertha Jane was going up to people and introducing herself.

I looked around for Thao. She was standing in the back of the room, hugging the fliers to her chest. I made my way through the people and went over to her.

"Who's that, Jason?"

"Huh?"

"Over there." She pointed toward the door where this guy had just come in. He had some people with him and they were all wearing buttons and they had a bunch of papers and cards they were handing out. A lot of people saw him and went over to him. They were talking real loud and I heard someone say "Good to see you, Elliot. You're going to give Blanton a real run for his money."

I turned to Thao. "That's Norman Elliot — he's running for mayor."

Thao looked kind of confused. We just stood there watching everything, and then a few minutes later another guy came in with about five people around him and the whole crowd just kind of parted as he walked in. I knew who he was from the papers and TV.

"Who's that, Jason?"

"Oliver P. Blanton — the mayor."

All the people with both Elliot and Mayor Blanton were buzzing around talking to everyone and handing out stuff. I wasn't sure exactly when Bertha Jane wanted us to hand out our stuff. I looked around and found her over in the corner and I went over to ask her about it. On my way through the crowd, I overheard two men talking.

"Well, we always have to give equal time to the flakes and the fringe candidates."

"And she's really related to Millard Fillmore. Isn't that a riot!"

They just cracked up. I felt my face get hot. I wanted to go over there and beat the crap out of them.

When I got to Bertha Jane, she was standing all alone. All the people were gathering around Mayor

Blanton and that guy Elliot. I hated seeing her alone like that.

"Bertha Jane, when do you want me to hand out the fliers?"

"I think after my speech would be a good time, dear."

"You don't think we should do it now?" I looked around. "I mean those other candidates are having their people hand out stuff." Even if the whole thing was crazy, I wanted us to act like everyone else.

"I think after they hear what I have to say would be best, Jason. They might be more apt to read it then." She looked toward the front of the room where they had long tables set up. The candidates were making their way up there and the president of the community club — Mrs. Chan, a real pretty lady in a business suit — was pounding the gavel. "I'd best be on my way up there, Jason. I'm supposed to speak last. Wish me luck!"

"Good luck, Bertha Jane. I'll pass out the stuff when you're done." I felt embarrassed for her, but I'd be damned if I'd let her know it.

"Thank you, dear."

She looked so little making her way up there all by herself — I was worried about the whole thing.

Thao and I found seats together in the back row and we listened as Mayor Oliver P. Blanton made his speech.

". . . We must keep up the good record and all that we have attained during my years as mayor. In my next term I plan to face the new challenges as we move ahead. We must take charge of our destiny and not step backwards, but move forward, taking control of our lives as we face the problems ahead. We will continue with strong fiscal management and taking care of human needs."

Everyone clapped for the mayor and then Norman Elliot had his turn.

". . . Let me say this about that. We can do better! It is time for a new consensus, a time for meeting the needs of all the people. I can bridge the gap with new fiscal responsibility and more for your tax dollars. It is time to get the city moving again. It is time to think about our future and our destiny and think about the issues at hand. We have a great city and my administration can make it greater."

Then everyone clapped a lot and then the next guy got up and said his name was Herman Watterton and his campaign slogan was "Watch Your Step!" He said he was running because he felt the pooper-scooper law was not being properly enforced and he started talking about the dog crap all over the place and how if he were the mayor the scoop law would be strongly enforced.

I heard people behind me whispering, "It's just the lunatic fringe now — might as well leave." Lots of people must have had that idea because the place started to clear out really fast. By the time Bertha Jane got up to speak there was only a handful left. Mayor Blanton and Norman Elliot left, too. They

179

said they had to go to other meetings that night. I looked over at Thao. She had the whole pile of fliers — a hundred of them — on her lap.

It didn't seem to bother Bertha Jane that most of the people had left. She went right up to the microphone and started her speech in this loud voice.

"My friends and neighbors . . . Today we live in a world where hope is a scarce commodity. We suffer from a loss of faith that anything good and constructive is still possible. We seem to have relinquished our efforts to make the world around us more humane in favor of controlling our own bodies. We witness this everywhere by the sorry emphasis on flattening our stomachs and obtaining thin thighs.

"But we must never give up trying to change the one terrible thing that hangs over all humankind — the Bomb. There must be no bombs.

"In order to renew our faith that things can be changed we must try to change a few little things. A very sad situation in the city of Seattle has been the death of the baby snow leopards at the zoo. The babies died because their mother was so disturbed by the sound of the hydroplane boat races on nearby Green Lake. Is it too much to ask that humans take this recreation to a lake away from the zoo, so that these innocent baby animals born in captivity, far away from their natural environment, can be saved?

"Another small but significant thing we can do in the city of Seattle is to encourage the use of live trees at Christmas time. When the season is over, these trees can be planted all over the city to help beautify

180

the environment. Christmas is a season that should be celebrated not by destruction — by the chopping down and later burning of a tree, one of the most beautiful creations of the universe. It should be celebrated by life itself — a living tree.

"I believe that through the small victories like saving the snow leopards and planting Christmas trees we can renew our faith that we can make a difference and we can be inspired to keep trying to eliminate the terrible destructive bombs man has invented . . . Save the snow leopards! Plant Christmas trees! No bombs!"

Bertha Jane sat down and Thao and I stood up and clapped like crazy. We just kept clapping and clapping. I looked around at the other people — they were clapping just like we were! I was so surprised — and proud! Bertha Jane was great. Those guys were jerks. *She was the best candidate!*

"Jason," Thao whispered, "I understood Bertha Jane's speech. It very good speech. But what other people say?"

"Dog shit."

"What?"

"The guy before Bertha Jane talked about cleaning up dog crap."

"What about other guys? What they say?"

"Nothing."

"Nothing?"

"That's right, Thao. Nothing."

CHAPTER 14

ON the way back from the Mt. Baker Community
Club, Bertha Jane told me that she wouldn't need me
to come to work until Monday afternoon. She said
she needed to get some rest so she'd be ready for the
rest of the campaign.

"Bertha Jane, I think we should do something with
those yard signs. I mean, we really need to get your
name around more."

"Oh my stars, Jason, I think I forgot all about
them, just my —"

"Your forgettery again." We both laughed.

"I have a little map of the city which shows the vacant lots where we can put them, Jason. Are the signs
still in the garage?"

"Uh-huh. I can drive around and put them up tomorrow, if you just tell me where you want them."

"That would be wonderful, Jason. I picked out

some vacant lots in six neighborhoods — Lechi, Madrona, Madison Park, Capitol Hill, Laurelhurst, and Queen Anne."

"We'll just blanket the city — right, Bertha Jane?"

"That's right, dear."

When we got to Bertha Jane's house I took the yard signs from the garage and put them in my car. Bertha Jane gave me the map. It had little circles on it where she wanted the signs.

"Thank you, Jason," she said, "I appreciate your enthusiasm."

"You're the best one, Bertha Jane."

On Saturday morning I got up early and drove around the city and put up the signs. The orange paint showed up real good. I thought the signs looked very nice.

I was hammering a sign in a vacant lot on Lake Washington Boulevard when Kenny drove by. He honked and waved out the window.

"Hey, Jason, what're you doing?"

"This is for the campaign."

"You mean that crazy old lady you work for is really running for mayor?"

I put the sign down and walked over to his car. "She's not crazy. She's a little eccentric, maybe. But she's the best candidate, Kenny."

"Are you getting paid to put up those signs?"

"No. I just want to."

"Kovak, you've flipped out. That old lady must have rubbed off on you."

"Yeah. She has." I grinned. I could have cared less if he thought I was nuts. "Well, I gotta finish these signs. See you later."

When I got back from my political work, the phone was ringing as I walked in the house. I ran to answer it.

"Hello."

"Mr. Jason Kovak?"

"Yes?" I squeaked, then I cleared my throat. I wondered if it was someone about the campaign.

"This is Detective Andy Rule. Seattle Police."

"Uh-huh."

"I have your name listed as a witness to a robbery at Wendy's on Mountainview Ave."

"Uh-huh."

"We'd like you to come down to headquarters at two thirty today. We have arrested a suspect and we'd like to see if you can make an identification."

"Oh."

"Mr. Kovak?"

"Uh-huh."

"We haven't been able to locate the other witnesses. No one answers the phone at the numbers we have for them so we've decided to go ahead with just your identification. We'd like to proceed with this as soon as possible."

"Oh."

"We're in the Public Safety Building right downtown on Third, between James and Cherry. Can you make it there, Mr. Kovak?"

"Oh — uh —"

"We need your help, Mr. Kovak."

"Oh, uh — okay, I guess."

"Take the elevator to the fifth floor, turn left, follow the sign to the phone, then pick it up and let us know you're there."

"Uh-huh."

"See you at two thirty, Mr. Kovak."

When I got off the phone, I was more nervous than I'd been in a long time. I had almost forgotten the robbery, what with working for Bertha Jane and all. Now the whole thing came back to me. Just the thought of looking at criminals was nerve-racking, but the prospect of actually identifying one freaked me out. I started pacing around my room. Maybe I could call the detective back and tell him I suddenly had to leave town.

What if that criminal figured out I was the one who put the finger on him and he got out of jail and came after me? I started sweating thinking about it. But I was just as scared not to show up — then the detective might come after me. I paced back and forth, worrying about all of this, and then it hit me. Not that long ago I was sitting tied up on the floor of the Wendy's storeroom looking at large mayonnaise jars believing I was one step away from the morgue. What I had thought about was not wanting to be a wimp. "Jason," I said to myself, "it's time to keep your promise."

"Right — starting tomorrow."

"Today — quit being a wimp today."

"I said I'd only try to quit being a wimp."

185

"That was a wimpy promise."

"But I'm scared."

"Think about Thao. She's brave. Think about all she's been through. Just go there anyway."

I went on like this just talking to myself back and forth, and I wondered all over again if I was flipping out. I had felt quite sane when I'd seen Kenny that morning, but maybe I really had gone totally nuts from the robbery and had a delayed reaction and now, at this very moment, the stress was catching up with me.

I kept on talking to myself like that and thinking about how brave Thao was the whole way to the Public Safety Building. When I got to Third and James Street, I was hoping that maybe I wouldn't be able to find a place to park and then I could just drive around the block forever and the detective would get tired of waiting so he'd decide to cancel the lineup. But it was Saturday. There were parking places everywhere.

I went into the Public Safety Building and took the elevator to the fifth floor. When I got off I was in this hallway with tan walls and asphalt tile on the floor. All I saw were a couple of bathrooms and a sign that said CRIMES AGAINST PERSONS, with an arrow pointing to the left. My heart started hammering. I followed the arrow and at the end of the hall there was a door with a phone on the wall next to it. It wasn't a phone with regular numbers on it, it just had this one button. I picked it up and pushed the button.

"Yes."

"Uh — I'm Jason Ko —"

"Speak up, I can't hear you."

"I'm Jason Kovak and —"

"Oh yes. Detective Rule is expecting you. He'll be right with you."

Then I heard a click, so I hung up. I was thinking that it might be a good time to go and get back on the elevator and go home, when the door next to the phone opened. A red-haired guy with a regular shirt and pants on came out and shook hands with me.

"Jason Kovak?"

"Uh-huh."

"I'm Andy Rule. Just follow me, son."

We went through the door down another hall and then through some double glass doors. There was a counter with a desk and a typewriter behind it. The detective got some forms out of the desk and explained the lineup to me. He handed me a form. It had eight circles in a row on it, all numbered. I was supposed to put an x through the circle that matched the position in the line of the man I thought was the robber. Then I was supposed to check either (1) I'm certain, (2) I can't be sure, or (3) None of the above. He told me he'd ask each man in the lineup to repeat a phrase that had been said during the robbery. Then he told me to wait for a few minutes.

I suppose it really was only a few minutes, but it seemed like hours before he came back.

"We're ready for you, Jason."

"Okay," I squeaked.

"Just follow me."

We went out through the double glass doors and then to a door marked Room 529. I followed him in. It was all dark like an auditorium. It had ten rows with about six seats across in each row. Detective Rule and I sat toward the back. I started shaking as soon as these eight men walked in all wearing these one-piece, blue-coverall-type clothes.

"They can't see you," Detective Rule said.

"Okay." I swallowed hard.

As I looked at the lineup, I thought about just checking "None of the above" for all the circles and getting out of there. But I looked over at Detective Rule — he seemed to be trying hard to catch these creeps. So I took a deep breath and decided that I should at least try to calm down and look carefully at each guy.

When I did that, they all looked alike. They all looked rotten. They were all white guys and they all had brownish hair and brown eyes. Detective Rule told me that they had only picked up one suspect and they were hoping to get the other suspect later that day.

He made them all stand to the side, and then to the back, and after that he had each one say, "I said, shut up." Their voices all sounded equally rotten, but there was one — the third guy from the left, something about him seemed familiar. I looked at his feet. He had on boots. They looked just like the boots of the guy that had kicked Henry. Remembering Henry getting kicked made me mad. I stared at the guy for a long time — I couldn't be sure about his face but his voice seemed right and so did his boots. I'd never forget those boots. I took the pencil Detective Rule had given me and I put an x in the third circle from the left. Then under it, I checked where it said "I can't be sure."

"Need any more time, son?"

"No." I handed the form to him and we left the auditorium.

"I'm sorry I couldn't be sure."

"That's okay, Jason. I appreciate your volunteering to come down here and help us out. That takes some guts."

"Yeah?"

"A lot of folks won't do it — don't want to get involved, you know. People are scared."

"Yeah, I guess some people might be." (Ha.)

Detective Rule held out his hand and shook hands with me again. He was nice. "Thanks for your time, son."

"Okay."

In the elevator on the way out of the building I thought my nervous stomach might be up to its old tricks and that I might throw up. I was still pretty scared. To take my mind off my stomach, I started whistling this song from one of my old Village People albums, "Macho Macho Man." It worked. I felt better when I did that and then I started singing it and I sang it all the way home. When I got home I went down to my room and got out the *Weekly* and read the ad from "Cheap Thrills" again.

Then I decided to press a few pounds with my

weight set. I got all the way up to 120 — I'd never done that much before and I said to myself, "Jason, today the police station, tomorrow — 'Cheap Thrills!' "

The rest of the weekend went great. I was down at McDonald's for breakfast on Sunday and I ran into Jill Washington. She was sitting at a table in the back talking to Henry. I guess he was on break or something. I went over to them.

"Hi, Jill. How's it going, Henry?"

"Hey, Jason. Sit down, man."

I pulled up a chair. "Did that police guy get a hold of you two?"

"Yeah, we had to go down there this morning." Jill said. "I think I'm still shaking. I was so scared."

"Yeah, I was, too. I had to go yesterday. Did you both go together?"

"Yeah, I think I would have told them to forget the whole thing if Jill hadn't been there," Henry said.

"I can't believe you did it all by yourself, Jason." Jill looked impressed. (I liked that very much.)

"Oh — no big deal." I laughed. "I was so scared I thought I'd dump my load!"

We laughed a lot and talked about the lineup. They had picked the same guy I did. Then we started talking about stuff at school.

"Everyone I know who goes to Ingraham is talking about the Homecoming dance. You going, Jill?" Henry asked.

"Nope."

"Too bad." Henry looked up at the counter. "Well,

guess I better get back to work." He started to get up.

"Why don't we go together?" I blurted that out.

"You and me, Jason? Or you and Jill? Or what?"

"You know a lot of people at Ingraham, Henry. All three of us — we can all go together — I'll pick you two up."

"Yeah, why not?" Jill smiled.

"Sounds good," Henry said. "Well, I'll catch you both later."

I stayed and talked some more to Jill. It was really nice. I felt great. And it was only just the beginning, because less than a week later, that next Saturday when I decided to check my box at the post office, there, sitting right in the box waiting, was a letter for T. Worthington Jones. I knew it had to be from "Cheap Thrills." I was on a roll!

I tore open the letter.

> *Dear Mr. Jones,*
> *For a good time meet me on Friday at 4:30 in the bar of Joe's Off Broadway. I'll have a flower in my hair.*
>
> *Sherrie Fileene*

That's all it said — I couldn't believe it. This was a woman of few words and, without a doubt, all action! Sherrie Fileene — what a name! Oh Sherrie, my chérie! I knew I wouldn't blow it this time. I was cookin'!

All week I studied my books getting ready for my date with her. I practiced amusing conversation every night, committing to memory dozens of one liners so I'd be totally prepared for the occasion.

191

While I was getting ready for bed Thursday night, the night before I was to meet "Cheap Thrills" herself, visions of sexy Sherrie danced in my head. I was sure I'd get another great dream out of the deal that night. And I was right. I did have a dream — but I wished I hadn't.

In the dream, I walked into the smoke-filled bar of Joe's Off Broadway. Everything was hazy and misty. There were shadowy figures at all the tables, beautiful people in fancy clothes. I hesitated at the door and gazed around the room, searching for Sherrie Fileene. Through the mist I noticed flower petals scattered across the floor. Slowly I followed them. Then, through the mist, at the end of the bar I saw a beautiful woman. Flowers were all around her. Moonlight streamed from a skylight, bathing her in silver. Her blond hair shimmered like spun gold. She looked across the room at me and smiled. My heart pounded. She looked like Christie Brinkley! I walked toward her through the mist. As I got closer and closer, her eyes were riveted to mine. As I was about to reach her, I lost sight of her. The mist became thick and rose up all around her. I knew I only had to take one more step and I would find her. Carefully, I stepped forward through the mist. I reached out to her. "Miss Fileene?"

She held her arms out to me. When I got to her the mist evaporated.

"Yeah?" She swiveled around on the barstool and gave me a big smile. She had a space between her front teeth and a mole on her chin with some black hairs growing out of it. She looked like the lady bowler, the cuddly woman, and "Cheap Thrills" all wrapped into one.

I turned, trying to run — but she grabbed me. "Are you the driver for T. Worthington Jones?"

"Uh-huh."

"Well, let's go, honey!" She leaped off the barstool.

"He's not here!"

"Well, then you can give little Sherrie a ride home." She grabbed my hand and pulled me out of the bar. We got in the Bentley. She directed me to an apartment building. I sped all the way. I couldn't wait to get rid of her. It was dark and there were bushes all around the parking lot. I stopped the car, waiting for her to get out.

Then she jumped me. She flew over from her side of the seat and jumped right on me.

"You're pretty cute, kid!" she panted and stuck her hand down my shirt and chewed on my ear and then pulled at my belt buckle. She was all over me — I was so squashed I could hardly breathe. She was kissing all over my neck and my face and slobbering all over me and I was gasping for air. Finally, I yanked my face away.

"I have a disease!" I yelled. "I have a disease!"

"Jason!"

"Huh — uh." I opened my eyes. It was Dad.

"Are you sick? I heard you yelling."

I rubbed my eyes and sat up in bed. Thank God it was Dad — and not that woman.

"I guess I just had a bad dream."

"You're sure you're okay?"

"Yeah. I'm fine."

"Maybe you ate something that didn't agree with you."

"I'm sure that was it."

"Well, if you're really okay, I guess I'll leave for work."

"Okay, Dad. Thanks."

After having the dream, I started worrying all morning about my meeting with Sherrie Fileene. What if she did turn out to be like that lady in the dream? But I decided to try some positive thinking. After all, I had those great dreams about Lisa LaRue and that had turned out terrible, so maybe since I had a nightmare about Sherrie Fileene, the real thing would turn out great. I sure hoped so.

I practiced my conversation all day when I was supposed to be doing assignments in class. At the end of the day I felt quite confident about it. I drove straight to Bertha Jane's house after school and she was ready to go to the doctor as soon as I got there.

On the way to the clinic Bertha Jane and I talked about the campaign. It was good to get my mind off Sherrie Fileene for a little while.

"Next time, is there any way you could get to make your speech first?" I asked. "I mean, all the people seemed to leave after Mayor Blanton and that guy Elliot talked and they didn't get to hear what a good speech it is."

"I don't think so, Jason. The major candidates usually speak first."

"I think you're a major candidate, Bertha Jane. I think you say better stuff than those guys."

"Well, Jason, my hope is just to plant a few seeds of a few ideas and if anyone voted for me, it would show that some people want to change things and make a difference."

"I think we should make some more signs."

"Well, we can see about that, dear."

I dropped Bertha Jane off at the clinic, watched her go in, and then drove to Madison and headed toward Broadway. I had read about this place where I was supposed to meet Sherrie Fileene. It was supposed to be this big singles place where all these beautiful people went to pick up each other. I wondered if it would look the way I pictured it in my dream. I put on my driver's hat, and went over my conversation once more in my head.

I drove up in front of Joe's Off Broadway. They had valet parking. A young guy with a white shirt and a tie on trotted out to the car.

"Can I park this for you, sir?"

"Uh, yeah, thanks."

"Bentley, isn't it?"

"Yeah."

"Some car." He opened the door for me and I got out and watched him drive it away. The entrance to the restaurant had this green canopy over it. "Jason," I said to myself, "you're on a roll — remember." I took a deep breath and went inside.

The bar was really crowded with all these guys in suits and the women looked like people in the windows of stores — they were all thin and bony and had on beautiful clothes and they had fancy hair. I stood in the doorway and looked around at all the tables.

In the back, at a table next to a window, was this blond lady with a big white flower in her hair. It had to be Sherrie Fileene.

My knees shook a little as I walked across the bar to her table.

"Miss Fileene?"

"Yes?" She looked up at me with a cheery smile. She didn't look like Christie Brinkley, but she didn't look like the lady in the dream, either. She was pretty and wearing a low-cut dress which I tried not to stare down into. Her blond hair was cut real short, like a crew cut but with some pieces sticking straight up. Some purple stuff was on her eyes and her lipstick was bright red. She was a little pudgy.

"I'm the driver for T. Worthington Jones and —"

"Oh, he's here!" She started to get up from the table.

"Well — no, actually, uh — do you mind if I sit down?"

"No, be my guest." She smiled.

"Thanks." I pulled out the chair and sat across from her.

"Where is he?" She leaned forward in her chair.

I tried not to look down her dress. "Well — you see, he got sick. Just a bad case of jet lag on his way back from France. He's not able to make it, but he sent me to tell you in person."

"Gee, that's too bad. He sounded like a fun guy.

You know, I really just put that ad in the paper for some laughs. I never thought anyone as interesting as T. Worthington Jones would answer."

"Uh-huh."

The waiter came up and asked what I'd like to order.

"I'll have a Coke. I never drink while I'm on duty."

The waiter left and Sherrie Fileene began looking around the room, probably trying to see if any other prospects were around so she could get some laughs. (It's now or never, Kovak.)

"You know, I once drank eight Cokes, but I burped Seven-Up."

She just kept looking around. Had she heard me? I looked out the window. On the sidewalk, I saw a couple pushing a baby stroller.

"You know the best way to drive a baby buggy is to tickle his feet," I said a little louder.

She just stared at me. "Waiter!" she called out, motioning to him. "I'll have another drink. I suppose I shouldn't — I'm on a diet — but I need one!"

"You know if you cheat on a diet, you gain in the end."

She glared at me.

I started sweating. "Uh — excuse me — I've got to go to the men's room."

I left the table, went in there, and took a leak. While I was washing my hands, I looked at myself in the mirror.

"Hang it up, Kovak. This isn't working."

"No argument. I'd rather be making real conversation with Thao and Bertha Jane. This whole thing is stupid."

"But how should I get out of this?"

"There are sixty ways to leave your lover — Jump on a blimp, wimp. Hit the road, toad. Fly like a bird, nerd."

"Oh great. But what should I say?"

"Good-bye."

But I wanted to say more than that. Why waste all those hours of practice? I should leave on a good note. So I thought about the advice in my books and decided to tell her that she was lovely and charming, that T. Worthington Jones would be disappointed, but that I needed to be on my way. I practiced that a few times and went back to the table.

She was sitting there sipping her drink.

"Miss Fileene —"

"Yeah."

"I gotta go."

"Good." She glared at me again. "But tell T.W. some other time."

"Yeah."

Outside the restaurant, I waited while the valet got the Bentley. He held the door and stood there while I got in. He just kept standing there. What did he want, anyway? Then it dawned on me. I was supposed to tip him. I got a dollar from my wallet, gave it to him, and drove off.

On the way to the clinic, I remembered I had left the driver's hat on the table with Sherrie Fileene. Who cares, I thought. I wouldn't need it again.

CHAPTER 15

BERTHA JANE looked kind of wobbly standing by the door of the clinic when I got back. I jumped out of the car to help her in.

"I feel silly, Jason. Needing you to lift me like this."

"You're not silly," I said, as I picked her up and helped her into the seat.

Actually, the truth of it was that I, Jason the Quick and the Brave, felt extremely silly and that whole stupid thing with Sherrie Fileene had cost me a dollar, too. I would have been better off if I had spent the whole time that I waited for Bertha Jane just staying in the Bentley reading Tintin books. Being a little kid has its advantages.

"Did you have a nice time while you waited for me, dear?"

"It was okay." (It was a joke.) I looked over at Bertha Jane. She was already sound asleep.

On the way home, I remembered something she had said to me during one of our long conversations. She said, "There's gold in your back yard." At the time I hadn't been sure what she meant. It just seemed like one of those things she said that was a little weird. But now I knew. The whole time I had been trying to get something going with those *Weekly* women, I had Bertha Jane and Thao right under my nose — my back yard, so to speak. They were real people. I could talk to them. It felt nice to think about that. Then I remembered I had another real thing about to happen in my life. Jill and Henry and I were going to the Homecoming thing together. That would be fun, and who knows — I might even get up the nerve to dance. Maybe I could dance with a real girl — like Jill or someone. Maybe even Karen Jacobsen would be there and I could handle her without throwing up. If I could survive that mess with Lisa LaRue and that stupid conversation with Sherrie Fileene, I could probably survive anything. Maybe I could ask more than one person to dance, even. I had practiced enough moves jumping around in the basement to MTV, that's for sure. But the more I thought about the dance, the more I realized I still wished Thao could have gone.

When we got home — I mean to Bertha Jane's house — I helped her in. She was so weak, I practically had to carry her in. Her little hat started to come off and when it did, I noticed something funny about her hair. It was kind of a reddish color, not white like it was supposed to be. Bertha Jane had on a wig. I guess I hadn't seen it before because she'd been wearing hats that covered it up.

I tried not to stare at the wig while I helped Bertha Jane up the stairs to her room but it really bothered me. I wanted to talk to Thao about it. I didn't feel like going home, just in case Bertha Jane might need me after her nap. So after she was in bed, I went all through the house looking for Thao. I finally found her in the den, working on her homework. It was raining outside and there was a fire in the fireplace. Josephine was curled up on Thao's lap and Thomas was lying on the hearth. I went over and crouched down next to him and patted him. He was such a good old dog — I really loved Thomas.

"Hi, Thao."

"Hi, Jason." Thao smiled. "How is Bertha Jane?"

"She's taking a nap. She's real tired."

Thao just nodded. Just then all the clocks went off — squawking and bonging and dinging and cuckooing all over the place.

"Thao, you know Bertha Jane is the best candidate." I talked real slow, while I scratched Thomas behind his ears. "I just wish she acted more normal — people might take her more seriously if she did, you know what I mean? I mean, I hated it when I heard people laughing at her at that meeting. And now she's even wearing a wig. It looks so stupid."

"Her hair fall out."

"Huh?"

"Her hair fall out. She have cancer."

201

I stood up.

"Cancer," she said real slowly, "Bertha Jane have cancer. She dying."

"No . . . No she doesn't . . ."

"She very sick."

"No . . ."

"Jason, she sick. Bertha Jane very sick."

". . .You don't know what you're talking about — She is not — You don't know anything! . . ."

"Jason — she —"

"YOU CAN'T EVEN SPEAK ENGLISH!"

I ran out of the den through the living room with all the pictures of those animals and all the clocks and all the flowers from the garden in the vases everywhere and that stupid picture of Millard Fillmore over the fireplace — everything went by like I was on a train. I heard Thomas bark as I yanked open the front door and ran down the driveway to my car. I just got in and took off. I didn't know where I was going but I drove like crazy all over. I didn't want to go home — I didn't know where to go — I just drove. Down McClellan to Rainier and then toward downtown and then on Jackson and then back toward the neighborhood and then I got on I-90 and on the floating bridge across Lake Washington and got off on Mercer Island. Just driving and driving all over the island on these winding roads and then back on the bridge again toward Seattle. It was raining hard. I put on the windshield wipers. I watched them go back and forth and back and forth across the window. At Seward Park I drove around and around the loop through the park just watching the wipers. Then I stopped the car and looked out at the water.

I pounded on the steering wheel. *How could I have not known!*

"Oh shit . . . Goddammit . . . *No!*"

I don't know what time it was when I finally got home. I went down to my room and sat in the dark listening to my stereo. The whole weekend was like that. I didn't feel like eating. I didn't feel like doing anything. I just slept. I tried to watch TV a few times but I'd just shut the damn thing off — even the Huskies game and the Seahawks game. The Hawks were playing the Raiders and usually I really get off on that, but I couldn't get into it. I just slept and listened to my stereo. The phone rang a few times but I wouldn't answer it.

Sunday night the phone rang again. I knew Dad must have been home and answered it because it stopped after a couple of rings.

"Jason!"

I didn't feel like saying anything.

"Jason!" Dad yelled down the stairs.

"What."

"Phone's for you."

"Tell 'em I'm busy."

I turned up the stereo and put on my earphones. When I looked up Dad was standing in the door of my room. I took off the earphones.

"Jason, there's some girl on the phone for you. I

can't understand her very well — a foreigner or
something — but she says she has to talk to you. She
sounds very upset. Jason?"

"What?"

"You didn't get some girl in trouble, did you?"

"Oh for God's sake —"

"What?"

"No!"

"Well, you better talk to her."

When Dad left I turned down the stereo and
picked up the phone.

"Jason?"

"Thao — I —"

"Bertha Jane is in hospital. She want to see you."

I couldn't say anything.

"Jason?"

I took a deep breath. "Uh-huh."

"Can you hear me?"

"Uh-huh — where? Where is she?"

"Same as clinic — Mason. Will you come?"

"Okay."

I hung up the phone and went to the bathroom
and splashed some cold water on my face. The last
time I had been in a hospital was when I was seven
and I broke my leg. Mom and Dad had both been
with me. I remembered Mom reading stories to me
and stuff and holding my hand a lot. A lot of my
friends wrote their names on my cast when I got
home — even though we were all in the second grade
and just learning how to write, but I remember all
those names and everyone drawing stuff all over it.

Even Mom — she made this little happy face on it smiling up at me. I was thinking about that cast as I left to go out to the car. Dad was in the kitchen.

"Jason? Where are you going?"

"To the hospital."

"What's wrong, son?"

". . . A friend — my friend is sick —"

The minute I said it I started crying. I just fell apart and Dad stood there — then he came over and put his arm around me. I grabbed him and held on to him real hard and he hugged me. I felt like a little kid. I just stood there like that in his arms, grabbing on to him and with him hugging me for a long time. I don't know how long it was before I stopped.

"Jason, is there anything I can do?"

"No — I gotta go." I wiped my face with the back of my arm. Dad still had his arm around me.

"Are you sure?"

Then I said, "Yeah, there is, Dad. There is something you can do. Just listen — just listen to me from now on, okay?"

"Okay, son."

Dad stood in the doorway and watched as I went out to my car.

I drove straight to Bertha Jane's house. I parked in her driveway and went around to the garden. I went to the rose garden. Bertha Jane loved those flowers. There were just a couple left in bloom. The last roses of autumn, she said they were. I picked them. Then I drove to the hospital.

I went up to the desk and asked what room to go to

for Bertha Jane Fillmore. They said 606. Then I got in the elevator and went up to the sixth floor. I felt like I was in a daze or underwater.

I walked down the corridor until I came to 606. When I looked in I saw Thao sitting next to Bertha Jane's bed. She was holding her hand. Bertha Jane had a lot of tubes in her — she looked so little and frail and she had on the wig. I felt like smashing all those tubes and everything in sight. I couldn't stand seeing her that way.

Thao looked up and saw me in the doorway.

"Jason." She bent over Bertha Jane. "Jason here, Bertha Jane."

I walked in and went over to Thao. I felt so bad when I saw her — it made me sick what I had said to her.

"Thao — about what I said . . . I'm sorry, Thao — I —"

"It okay, Jason."

"I just —"

"Jason, it okay," she said softly.

Bertha Jane opened her eyes. I showed her the roses. She gave me a little smile and I went around and sat on the other side of the bed. I held her other hand.

"Thank you, Jason," Bertha Jane whispered. She could hardly talk so I had to bend very close to her to hear. She spoke slowly, as if it was a struggle to get out each single word. "You mustn't worry about me. I have had a rich life, filled to the brim with work and love. And I'm quite ready to let go of it . . ." Then she motioned to her cane next to the bed. "Open it, dear," she whispered.

I unscrewed the top and took out a rolled-up piece of paper.

Dear Jason,

After I'm gone Thao will have a new sponsor in California, near her uncle who came here six months ago. Thao and I have talked about this and she would like to be near him. I've made all the arrangements and have left enough money to take care of her. Please help her get there safely. Also, dear, I'd like you to have Josephine and Thomas. I know you would be good to them.

We are all orphans, Jason, long before our parents die, because we must claim the loneliness of adulthood and learn to parent ourselves.

We can comfort ourselves by finding pleasure and meaning in each moment by looking to the joy and peace that the beauty all around us can provide. And especially, we can comfort ourselves through the love we have for one another.

We must do all we can about despair and suffering, but its existence does not negate the song of the black-capped chickadee or the loveliness of a golden autumn morning. Be happy, Jason. My love goes with you.

Your friend,
Bertha Jane

I folded up the paper. "Bertha Jane —" I bent close to her cheek. "Bertha Jane — I love you, Bertha Jane."

She couldn't talk anymore, but I felt her squeeze my hand. Thao and I sat there holding Bertha Jane's hands. It was dark outside. At eleven she died.

When I got home from the hospital Dad was gone. I went down to my room and found the poem about listening that Bertha Jane had given to me. I took it up to Dad's room and put it on his dresser. I hoped Bertha Jane was right — I hoped he could just listen.

It was raining on Tuesday when I went over to Bertha Jane's house to help Thao pack. Usually, I don't think about the rain much, but it seemed like the clouds were crying. At her house, Thao said a man from the bank and Bertha Jane's lawyer had been there that morning and they would be taking care of the house and all of Bertha Jane's things, and settling her estate after Thao left.

"I have more things now than when I came here, Jason," she said. "Bertha Jane give me so much. I have nothing but the clothes I wear when I come. Now what to do?"

"I can get a suitcase for you from my house."

"How I give it back to you, Jason?"

"You can keep it."

"Maybe you come visit me in California, get suitcase then?"

I smiled, and it felt strange. Even though Bertha Jane had died only a couple of days ago, it felt like I hadn't smiled in a long time. "I'd like that a lot."

"Maybe you meet uncle."

"I'd like to meet your uncle."

"I feel *may man*, Jason — real lucky to have Bertha Jane for sponsor."

I couldn't say anything. I thought I might lose it again. I didn't want to fall apart in front of Thao, but I knew she could tell I was shook up.

"Maybe it easier for me, Jason. I sad, I feel big hurt inside me, but I lose many people in my life. I just feel lucky for time I had with Bertha Jane Fillmore."

I nodded.

"Jason, you my first American friend."

I couldn't talk very well.

Then the whole thing got me. "It's funny, Thao. I was supposed to help you talk and right now I can't say much — but you're doing fine."

"You good teacher, Jason."

"You too, Thao." She didn't seem to know what I meant when I said that, but I figured maybe I could write her about the stuff she and Bertha Jane had taught me. It would be a real letter, from me, Jason Kovak. "I'll go home and get the suitcase," I said.

"Okay. When you take Josephine and Thomas?"

"I want to buy some dog food and some cat food and have everything all ready for them, so I think I'll get them late tonight after I get back from taking you to the airport."

"They be happy with you, Jason."

"I hope so. I'm pretty sure Dad will like them. He and I and my brother, Jeff — we always wanted animals, but Mom hated them so we never had any." I patted Josephine on my way out. "Well, I guess I better get that suitcase."

I'd left Thao and started driving to my house when I noticed American flags all over the place and people standing on the corners with signs. It dawned on me what day it was.

I drove as fast as I could back to Bertha Jane's house and ran up to the door.

"Thao!"

"Jason, you get suitcase so soon?"

"Thao, listen. I know you have to pack and everything and I'll help you — but right now there is something we have to do."

"What, Jason?"

"Just come with me."

"Okay."

Thao got her coat and came to my car. I drove as fast as I could through the neighborhood and parked in front of John Muir School where there was a polling place.

I jumped out of the car and went around and opened the trunk. I took out this huge sign I had made after the meeting at the Mt. Baker Community Club. Thao helped me carry it and we went to the street corner and stood there in the rain under the streetlight holding it while all the cars went by.

It started raining harder and we stood there like that in the rain holding the sign.

VOTE FOR BERTHA JANE FILLMORE
SAVE THE SNOW LEOPARDS
PLANT CHRISTMAS TREES
NO BOMBS